EVEN THE UNKNOWN
W~~~~~~~~~~~~~~EM

D0103623

#1

Extreme Zone—where your nightmares become reality.... Noah and Harley were thrown together by circumstances beyond their control. Now they are bound together by forces beyond their comprehension. They must be careful whom they trust, for Noah and Harley have crossed the dark borders of the Extreme Zone, and anyone could lead them to certain doom—or to salvation.

**SEND IN TWO COMPLETED OFFICIAL ENTRY FORMS
AND RECEIVE A FREE
EXTREME ZONE BASEBALL CAP!**

Official Entry Form:

Name_____Birthdate_____

Address_____

City_____State_____Zip_____

Phone_____

An Archway Paperback
Published By Pocket Books

1293 (1 of 2)

ARCHWAY PAPERBACKS

EXTREME ZONE #1

PROOF OF PURCHASE OFFER

OFFICIAL RULES

1. To receive your free EXTREME ZONE baseball cap (approximate retail value: $8.00), submit this completed Official Entry Form and at least one Official Entry Form from either books 2, 3, or 4 (no copies allowed). Offer good only while supplies last. Allow 6-8 weeks for delivery. Send entries to the Archway Paperbacks/EZ Promotion, 13th Floor, 1230 Avenue of the Americas, NY, NY 10020.

2. The offer is open to residents of the U.S. and Canada. Void where prohibited. Employees of Simon & Schuster, Inc., its parent, subsidiaries, suppliers, affiliates, agencies, participating retailers, and their families living in the same household are not eligible. One EXTREME ZONE baseball cap per person. Offer expires 12/31/97.

3. Not responsible for lost, late, postage due or misdirected responses. Requests not complying with all offer requirements will not be honored. Any fraudulent submission will be prosecuted to the fullest extent permitted by law.

"Someone tried to run me down last night on the way home," Noah told Harley.

"*What?*" Harley stared at him with her mouth hanging open.

Noah took a deep breath. "I think it has to do with my dreams."

"Dreams?" Harley asked. "How can dreams have anything to do with someone wanting to kill you?"

"I'm going to tell you this as flat as I can," Noah said. "When I'm done, you can tell me I'm nuts. I don't care."

"All right," said Harley. She shifted in the car seat. "Go ahead."

Noah nodded. "The dreams began about three weeks ago." He went on to describe the glowing faces with their huge dark eyes, the human doctor, the flashing knife, and the terrible fear that accompanied the mysterious and horrifying images.

"Okay," Harley said. "You've been having weird dreams about little guys with big heads. They're still just dreams. How can this have anything to do with someone trying to run you over?"

"Because I don't think they're just dreams," Noah replied.

"What else could they be?"

"Memories."

"Memories of what?" Harley asked.

Noah ran a hand through his floppy hair. "Of an abduction."

Don't miss the next books in this thrilling new series:

Available from ARCHWAY Paperbacks

E☒TREME ZONE

N I G H T
T E R R O R S

M . C .   S U M N E R

AN ARCHWAY PAPERBACK
Published by POCKET BOOKS
New York   London   Toronto   Sydney   Tokyo   Singapore

AN ARCHWAY PAPERBACK *Original*

 An Archway Paperback published by
POCKET BOOKS, a division of Simon & Schuster Inc.
1230 Avenue of the Americas, New York, NY 10020

Produced by Daniel Weiss Associates, Inc., New York

Copyright © 1997 by Daniel Weiss Associates, Inc., and
Mark C. Sumner
Cover art copyright © 1997 by Daniel Weiss Associates, Inc.

ISBN: 0-671-00241-4

First Archway Paperback printing February 1997

10 9 8 7 6 5 4 3 2 1

AN ARCHWAY PAPERBACK and colophon are registered trademarks of Simon & Schuster Inc.

Printed in the U.S.A.

IL 7+

PROLOGUE X

He woke up screaming.

In that first moment, he could still feel the straps around his arms and the cold metal table at his back. He could see blurry figures surrounding him in the darkness, their huge, black eyes set in bloated faces of featureless white.

But the room was only his own bedroom. The straps around his limbs were only sheets, twisted and tangled. The ghostly faces were only the rows of maps and papers he had taped against the walls. There was no one else in the room.

For long minutes he sat in the darkness, feeling the cold sweat of fear roll down his face. The same sweat had plastered his T-shirt over the muscles of his chest, making the air icy against his skin. Slowly, his breathing returned to normal.

Finally, the fear receded, leaving behind images and memories that grew more vague with each passing second. The whole thing *was* ridiculous. He was being frightened by *dreams,* nothing more. He ran a hand across his floppy, damp hair, lay down, and closed his eyes.

The images were still there, waiting for him. White faces. Black eyes. The gleam of a knife, stabbing downward. He tried to think of something—anything—that would clear those visions from his mind. But even after an hour of tossing and turning, sleep would not come. He lay there with the images

1

running through his head, images of darkness and light. And terror.

"It's only a dream," he whispered. He kept his eyes stubbornly closed. Finally, he fell into a groggy, restless doze.

While he lay there, thin lines of red light slipped through the venetian blinds on the windows, momentarily filling the room with a ruddy, pulsing light. Outside the house, a ball of bloodred fire, four feet across, hovered in the air beside the bedroom window. It bobbed above the ground like a balloon on an invisible string, swaying slightly in the night wind. Abruptly, it rose to the level of the rooftop and then began to move away, casting its red light over the sleeping neighborhood. In moments, the ball of fire had vanished behind a copse of trees.

Inside the bedroom, the dreamer pulled the pillow over his head and moaned.

ONE

Harley Davisidaro stopped and put down her right foot to balance the weight of her 880 Sportster motorcycle. She looked enviously at the people walking along the sidewalks of Stone Harbor. Much as she loved her bike, after riding twelve hours a day for four days in a row, she was more than ready to get off and walk.

The radio in her helmet crackled. "You okay?" asked her father, his voice tinny in the helmet's small speakers.

"Yeah," Harley replied. "I'm fine." She pushed her helmet's face shield up and waved at her father's car, which was stopped two vehicles ahead at the light.

"Hang in there, kid," said the voice on the radio. "Almost home."

"Sure," Harley replied.

Ever since she had gotten her motorcycle, she had dreamed of driving it across the country. The idea had seemed romantic: the open road, the wind in her hair—all that stuff. But now, that romantic idea was gone. There had been wind in her hair, all right, but also bugs in her teeth and major soreness in her rear. Her legs and back felt as if they had been pounded by sledgehammers.

As she waited at the light, Harley stared at the small seaside town around her. Stone Harbor was not exactly a cheery sight. The buildings were old and low, with thick stone walls and steep roofs designed to ward off centuries of hurricanes and cold East Coast winters. On the nearest door was a sign that read Closed for the Season. It wasn't the only one. A good half of the stores looked closed or empty. There wasn't a McDonald's or Blockbuster Video store in sight.

The light changed and traffic moved on. Harley followed her father's white government-issue car out of town. They continued down a two-lane road, weaving through hills hugged by a dense forest of oak and ash. It was probably pretty in summer, but now the winter trees looked like black skeletons on the hillsides.

Ten minutes of driving brought them to a desolate road on a hill twice as tall as any other nearby. Just ahead, a tall fence topped by loops of gleaming razor wire wove between the trees, and a sliding gate blocked the road. A sign off to the side displayed black letters on a plain white background: Tulley Hill Research Facility. Authorized Personnel Only. Below that was another sign: Trespassers Subject to Immediate Execution. That's new, Harley thought as she pulled up next to her father's car. And awfully severe. She hadn't seen a sign like that even when her father was working at a top-secret base in Nevada.

A pair of guards emerged from a small blockhouse and headed for the car. They wore odd, smooth blue uniforms and hard white helmets stamped MP. One of them had broad shoulders and the heavy arms and legs of a weight lifter. The other one was more slender, with sharp features and a clipboard clutched in his hands. Both of them had guns at their belts. Harley's father rolled down his window and handed a sheaf of papers to the clipboard guy. The other guard watched with narrowed eyes.

Harley pulled off her own helmet and shook out her hair while she waited for the guards to finish looking at her father's papers. In her opinion, Tulley Hill Research Facility didn't look like much. Edwards Air Force Base, where her father had worked last, had been a huge, busy place. Harley could see nothing at Tulley Hill but the road continuing on through the trees. There were no jets roaring overhead, and no military people lined up to get in and out of the base. The guards finished talking to Harley's father and walked over to the motorcycle. Weight Lifter walked in front, the bunched muscles of his shoulders straining the fabric of his uniform. As soon as he got a good look at Harley, the guard's lips turned up in a smile. "Good afternoon," he said.

Harley smiled back cautiously. A lot of the guys on the bases were only eighteen or nineteen, and starved for female company. Harley had learned years earlier that she had to be careful not to encourage them. If Harley gave the soldiers the wrong signals, she could be fighting them off for as long as she was there.

The clipboard carrier approached. From the serious, officious look on his razor-thin features, Harley knew she wasn't going to have any trouble with *him* getting too friendly. Clipboard glanced once at Harley, then looked down at his papers. "You Kathleen Elise Davisidaro?"

Harley tucked her helmet under her arm and

nodded. "That's what it says on my driver's license," she answered. "But everyone calls me Harley."

"Harley," Weight Lifter said. "I like that."

"Let's just see that license," Clipboard instructed coldly.

"Sure." Harley fished her driver's license out of one of the bags strapped to the bike and handed it to the guard. The MP looked at the card, at Harley, then back at his clipboard. From the pinched expression on his face, he might as well have been cataloging army blankets.

Finally he took a red plastic card and handed it to Harley. "This is your identification while you are with this facility. You must have this card on your person at all times. If you are found without your card, you might never get the chance to correct your error. Is that clear?"

Harley nodded. She could read between the lines: Being caught inside Tulley Hill without a pass card could get you shot. She figured that he was exaggerating, but even so, this place was starting to give her the creeps.

"Take the card and sign in here," said the guard.

Harley took the red plastic rectangle from Clipboard's hand. It looked more like a credit card than a security pass. There was a line of numbers along one side and some kind of bar code tucked into the corner. On the other side of the card was a color photo of Harley. Seeing it gave her a chill.

"Where did you get this picture?" she asked. She'd never seen the photo before. She'd never posed for it, either.

"Sign," repeated Clipboard.

Harley signed.

The guard nodded. "Remember: Carry this identification with you at all times."

"Right," Harley replied.

The weight lifter gave Harley another smile as the two walked away, but she barely noticed. Between the behavior of the guards and the unfamiliar photo, Harley felt spooked. Tulley Hill was definitely not like the other places she had lived with her father.

The metal gate slid open and her father's car rolled through. Harley shoved her helmet back onto her head and followed.

The road inside the base was narrow, and the bare trees leaned out to cast black, twisted shadows across the pavement. Harley turned a corner, and a series of ten ranch houses appeared from the woods. They were brick, with square lawns of dead brown grass. Harley's father turned the car into the driveway of the last house, and Harley followed his lead. She pulled the motorcycle up against the rear bumper of the car, pushed down the kickstand, and killed the engine. Her legs shaking with relief, she climbed off the bike.

Her father smiled at her as he came out of the car. "What do you think?" he asked. "This sure beats the place at Edwards, huh?"

"I guess," Harley replied, glancing up at the prefab house. The old place had been just an apartment shoved in among hundreds of others.

Her father's expression turned to puzzlement. "What's wrong, kiddo? I thought you'd be impressed.

This is the first time we've had a real house in years."

"The house is great," said Harley. "It's just this base." She shrugged. "Don't you think it's kind of weird?"

"I told you before that Tulley's not a regular military base," her father replied. "It's a joint facility run by Unit 17."

Harley nodded. "I remember." Until her father took this job, she had never heard of Unit 17. They were supposed to be some kind of military intelligence agency, but what they really did wasn't clear to Harley.

"With U17 in charge," her father continued, "the protocol here's bound to be a little different than what we're used to. Give it a chance, okay?" He smiled again.

Even though he was on the high side of forty, Frank Davisidaro had jet black hair and a brilliant white smile that shone in contrast to his tan skin. Ever since she was a little girl, Harley had been helpless against her father's smile.

"Okay," she said, returning his grin grudgingly. "Let's see what the house is like on the inside."

The red security cards turned out to be more than simple identification. The only way to get the door open was by sliding the card into a slot below the latch. Inside, the house was filled with soft cream-colored carpeting and light-wood furniture that looked brand-new. There were paintings on the walls of abstract pastel shapes. The interior looked like a suite in a good hotel—tasteful, expensive, and lifeless.

"What do you think?" asked Harley's father. "Quite a step up."

Harley dumped her helmet on a mushroom-colored couch. "I guess." She ran her hand over the white countertop separating the living room from the kitchen. "Seems kind of cold, though."

"They've probably got the heat turned down," said her father.

"Not that kind of cold," Harley corrected him. "*Cold*, like no one's ever lived here."

Her father rubbed his chin and looked around the room. "It does look a little *too* perfect, doesn't it? Well, I've no doubt you'll take care of that. A week from now you'll have your underwear hanging in the shower and motorcycle magazines all over the couch."

Harley grinned. "That won't take a week." Then she glanced at her watch. "I need to get back to town and register for school." She took a deep breath, and slowly exhaled. "Another chance to be the new girl in town."

Her father brushed his hand lightly against Harley's cheek. "I know you don't like being dragged all over the country. And I know it's been especially hard on you since . . . your mom passed away. . . ." Mr. Davisidaro's voice caught for a moment, but then he rushed on. "Just remember that this is a big project. *The* big project. Once we get this one down, we'll be able to make our own choices."

"Sure," said Harley. Her father was all the family she had left. She hated the idea of being away from him, but she wished he would take a job that would let them stay in one place for more than a few months. It would be good to be able to make friends without knowing she was going to lose them with the next move.

"I better run," she said, retrieving her helmet. "School's probably already let out."

"Don't forget your pass card."

"Of course," Harley replied. "Wouldn't want to be shot for forgetting my plastic."

The guards waved her through on her way out and in a moment she was roaring back toward Stone Harbor. Stone Harbor High School was masked by a screen of huge, towering elms that had to be older than the country. Even without leaves, the heavy branches of the trees locked together in a wall of dark wood. Behind the old trees was a wide two-story stone-and-brick structure—a building that looked almost as old as the ancient trees.

Harley glanced at her watch. Four o' clock. A few cars were still rolling out of the parking lot. She parked her bike and started up the steps to the school.

Before she could get to the top, four students came out in a laughing, talking knot. There were two girls and two guys, all wearing the same blue-and-gray jackets. The girls were both blond and had fading summer tans. The two guys were a mixed pair—one short with dark hair, one very tall and blond—but both had the same confident manner. They walked down the steps like they were the kings and queens of the town.

The dark-haired guy gave Harley a good look as

they went past. For a second it seemed as though he were going to say something to her, but the girl at his side tugged him away. Her motorcycle drew considerably more attention. Both of the guys stopped to look at the bike, and an admiring whistle drifted up the stairs.

"That your bike?"

The voice came from above. Harley looked up and saw a short girl with shoulder length auburn hair and round glasses.

"Yeah," Harley replied.

"Cool," the girl said. She looked Harley up and down. "You in a gang or something?"

Harley blinked. "Um . . . no. I just have a motorcycle. That doesn't make me some outlaw biker."

"That's too bad," said the short girl. "This town could use a few outlaws." She gave an elaborate sigh. "Once the summer is over, this place is about as interesting as a rock." She sighed again. "And that's an insult to rocks."

Harley laughed. "It can't be that bad."

"Just wait and see," the girl warned. All at once her frown disappeared and was replaced by a friendly, infectious grin. "Hi," she said. "I'm Dee Janes." She stuck out her hand.

Harley pumped the girl's hand. "Harley Davisidaro."

"Harley. Cool." Dee shook her head. "Why is it everybody gets a good name but me?"

"Mine's not that good," said Harley. "It's really Kathleen. Harley's just a nickname."

"Kathleen?" Dee wrinkled her nose and stuck out

11

her tongue. "Stick with Harley. It suits you better."

"I've always thought so." Harley found herself smiling broadly. "Maybe we can make up a new name for you."

"Maybe," said the girl. "But I think I'm hopelessly stuck being a Dee."

More laughter drifted up from the group at the bottom of the stairs. One of the guys ran his hands over the motorcycle's seat. Before Harley could tell him to lay off, the whole group moved on.

"How about those guys," Harley asked, tilting her head in the direction of the departing group. "Who are they?"

Dee's frown reappeared. "The guys are on the basketball team. The girls are cheerleaders. They're all popular and most of them are rich. Sickening, isn't it?"

"Pretty much," Harley said with a nod.

"Worse than that," said Dee. She crossed her arms and scowled down at the laughing students. "Neither of those guys ever asked me out."

Harley laughed again. "How about showing me where the office is?" she asked. "I need to sign up."

"You're going to school here? Cool."

"*Cool.* You say that a lot, don't you?"

Dee nodded. "Yep, and don't expect me to stop. Come on. I'll show you where the chief prison warden sits."

As they reached the top of the stairs, the door was suddenly thrown open so hard it struck Harley in the shoulder and sent her stumbling back. The heel of her boot slipped over the top step. She whirled her arms in the air, fighting for balance. A fraction of a second before she fell down the steps, a hand shot out and grabbed her by the wrist.

"Are you all right?"

Harley looked up to see a guy standing over her. Despite the cold weather, he wore loose khaki pants and a slouchy T-shirt that accentuated his long, tautly muscled arms and broad shoulders. But that wasn't what really caught Harley's attention. What she saw first was a pair of incredibly deep blue eyes flecked with gray.

"You all right?" he asked again.

Harley nodded. "I think so."

The guy let go of her wrist. "Sorry," he said. "I didn't mean to hurt you. I was just . . ." He stopped and looked hard into Harley's eyes. "You're sure you're okay?"

"Yeah," Harley answered. She smiled back. "I'm fine."

Dee stepped around Harley and jabbed a finger into the guy's lean chest. "No thanks to you, Templer," she scolded. "There are other people in this school, you know." Her voice was stern, but there was a grin on her face.

The tall guy looked down at Dee. For a moment, his face was tight with some emotion Harley couldn't name. But then he gently shook his head and smiled back faintly. "You going to give me a ticket, Officer Janes?" he asked Dee.

"Only a warning," Dee bantered back. "But you better watch it."

"Absolutely." The guy looked back at Harley.

Again, he hesitated momentarily. "I guess I better go before Dee changes her mind," he said finally. With that, he slipped past Harley and hurried down the stairs. As soon as he hit the sidewalk, he took off, running at a speed that was almost a sprint.

Dee planted her hands on her hips. "He's not usually in such a hurry."

"Who is he?" Harley asked. She watched the tall, slender figure lope across the school's front lawn.

"Noah Templer," Dee replied. "Basketball star, track star, straight-A student. You name it, he's won it."

Harley followed Noah with her gaze as he ran down the lane of old trees. "He seems different from the others," she said softly.

Dee nodded. "Noah always has been. Just because he can put a ball through a hoop, he doesn't think he's the hottest thing this side of the sun. He even dated me for a while, if you can believe that."

"Really?" Harley asked. "Why did you break up?"

"We decided we made better friends," Dee replied. She sighed. "Actually, I think *he* decided. I was already planning the wedding. It's really too bad about Noah."

Harley frowned. "What's too bad?"

Dee held a finger up beside her head and circled it around. "Everybody says he's gone nuts," she said. "Fruit loops. Bonkaroonie."

"Do you believe that?"

"I don't know," Dee said with a shrug. "He hasn't been talking to me lately. Hasn't been talking to anyone. He's getting in trouble with the teachers, too. It seems like he doesn't do anything but stare off into space." She sighed again. "Come on. Let's get to the office before someone else knocks you down."

Harley nodded, but she stayed where she was for a moment longer, watching Noah Templer disappear among the huge old trees. There was something in his bright blue eyes—a kind of light that Harley had never seen before. Maybe it meant that he was crazy, but somehow she didn't think so.

What Harley thought was that Noah Templer was very cute—and that he was scared to death.

Noah pushed open the door of the Stone Harbor Library and rushed into the cool shadows inside. Quickly, he shut the door. Then he spun around and pressed his face to the glass, trying to see who was following him.

Outside, a woman walked down the sidewalk with a white bakery box cradled in her arms. Two small children raced past, laughing as they ran. A stray dog wandered around the corner of the courthouse and hurried across the street to vanish in a narrow alley. That was all.

There was no one following Noah. There never had been.

"Dreams," he whispered to himself. "They're only dreams."

Noah wished he had his car. Ever since ninth grade, he had run back and forth to his home every day. Even when everyone started getting their driver's licenses and the other guys brought their cars to school to show off, Noah kept on running. It helped him keep in shape, and it gave him time to think. But now it didn't seem like such a good idea. Every moment he was outside, he felt like a germ under a microscope. He felt *watched*.

Noah's heartbeat returned to normal as he walked between the tall shelves of books. Lately the library was the only place where he really felt safe. He didn't feel safe at school. School was too full of people who kept asking questions that Noah couldn't answer. He certainly didn't feel safe at home. Home was where they came and. . . .

Even in the cool, safe corridors hidden between the bookshelves, Noah felt a wash of fear. "Dreams," he whispered again. Nothing had happened at home. Nothing bad, anyway. It was all in his dreams.

Noah nodded to the gray-haired librarian who was sitting behind her desk, and then headed for the shelves at the back of the main room. There, hidden between rows of books about the Bermuda Triangle, Sasquatch, and the Loch Ness Monster, were the handful of volumes that Noah was after—the books about unidentified flying objects. *UFO's.*

He dragged a small stool over and sat down. After pulling a notebook from his backpack, Noah took down one of the books from the shelf and began to scan through the chapters. He had already read most of the UFO books in the library's small collection, but the first time he had flipped through them, Noah had not yet organized his project. Now he knew what to look for.

Noah turned pages until he came across an interesting case. He quickly scribbled down the information in a small notepad. "Womford, New Hampshire. Female. 26. August 1992."

The information seemed a little familiar. It was likely that Noah had seen this same case in another book, or maybe he had gotten it off some page on the World Wide Web. The cases that sounded good got reprinted a lot. It didn't matter. Once he entered the data into his computer, he could count on his database to sort out the duplicates.

A slim finger suddenly reached down and flicked the cover of the book closed.

Startled, Noah looked up and saw Caroline Crewson staring down at him with a frown on her pretty face. "I *thought* it was you I saw running past me," she said.

"I'm sorry," said Noah. "I didn't even see you."

Caroline crossed her arms in front of her chest. "You don't see anything these days, do you? Nothing but your flying saucers and your little green men."

A mixture of embarrassment and anger boiled in Noah's guts. When the dreams had started, he had told Caroline all about them. After all, he'd been dating her at the time, and he had trusted her. Love will do that to you, Noah thought cynically. It made me stupid. Her reaction had been so strongly negative that Noah never had mentioned the dreams to anyone else—not even Dee, who he had considered telling at one point. Caroline had laughed in his face. There was *no way* he was going to risk a response like that again.

"I should never have told you anything," he said sullenly to Caroline. "And I *never* said they were green."

"Oh, of *course* not." Caroline rolled her eyes. "Come *on,* Noah. When are you going to forget all this stupid UFO stuff and start acting like a normal person again?"

Noah narrowed his eyes, glaring at her. "Why should *you* care?" he asked.

Caroline shrugged, sending a ripple through her

chestnut brown hair. Her face softened. "I miss you," she said quietly. "I thought maybe we could start going out again."

Noah rose to his feet. "After you told everyone at school that I was *crazy?*" Anger was running through him now like a red-hot cable. He shook his head furiously. "What makes you think I'd *want* to see you again?"

Caroline's red lips turned up in a snarl. She opened her mouth to reply, but before she got a word out, the librarian appeared at the end of the aisle.

"Quiet, please," she hissed. The woman looked at the two students with obvious disapproval. "If you must argue, please don't do it in the library."

Caroline's green eyes were still locked on Noah's face. "Don't worry," she said through her teeth. "I'm done talking to him."

The librarian looked at them for a moment longer, then moved away down an aisle.

"You're even crazier than I ever thought," Caroline said. Her voice was only a whisper, but her words still stung. She tossed back her hair, turned on her heel, and stomped away, following the librarian down the aisle.

"I'm *not* crazy," Noah said softly. Even to his own ears, it sounded lame.

Caroline stopped and looked at him over her shoulder. She laughed. "Tell it to the little green men." With that she walked around the end of the aisle and disappeared. A few seconds later, Noah heard the ring of the bell over the library door as Caroline left.

Noah looked down at the book in his hands. The cover showed a huge disk hovering over a frightened woman. In huge bright green letters, the title screamed a warning of a secret invasion. Before the dreams, he wouldn't even have thought about picking up this book.

"Maybe I really am crazy," Noah whispered to himself.

He flipped open the book, looking for the case he had been writing down before Caroline had interrupted. Instead he found himself looking at a sketch of a flat, oval face with large black eyes. The image shocked him as if he'd grabbed the end of a live electric line.

Noah staggered back against a bookshelf. All around him, the library dimmed. An uninflected, toneless voice spoke in his ear.

"Almost finished."

Noah looked around and saw a ring of pale faces leering down at him. He wanted to move. He wanted to scream. But he couldn't even blink.

There was a flash above him. Light glimmered from the side of a shining metal blade. The scalpel plunged down.

There was a tug on Noah's arm.

"Hey," said a new voice. "Hey. You can't remove that book from the library without checking it out first."

Noah blinked. He was standing by the door of the library with the UFO book still clutched in one hand. Close behind him was the librarian.

"Are you going to check that out?" she asked sternly.

"No," replied Noah softly. He held out the book.

20

"No. I don't think so." The librarian took the book. She gave him one last hard look and then marched back to her place behind the desk.

Noah slipped out of the library and breathed in the cool air, trying to slow his heartbeat. The anger he had felt while talking to Caroline was gone. In its place was nothing but fear.

He couldn't remember getting up and walking to the front of the library, but obviously he had. He was suddenly very relieved that he hadn't driven his car to school. Having a blackout while behind the wheel seemed like a really bad idea.

All around him, Stone Harbor looked the same as always. The October sky was gray, and it would probably rain soon. But for the moment people were walking back and forth on the sidewalks, going in and out of stores, carrying packages—being normal.

Noah turned and started running toward home. Almost at once he had that terrible feeling again. The feeling of being *watched*. This time he refused to turn around. There was no one behind him, and he was not about to start jumping at shadows. Gritting his teeth, Noah clamped down on his fear and hurried around the corner.

Halfway down the next block, a bright red Camaro pulled over to the curb just in front of Noah. It paced him as he ran, keeping a few yards ahead. After a few seconds, the window on the driver's side rolled down and Josh McQuinn stuck his head out.

"Hey," called Josh. Even in the gray afternoon light, Josh's hair was so pale it seemed to glow. "Where you heading?"

Noah tried to work up a smile in return. "Just going home."

"Well, hop in, man. I'll give you a ride."

"That's okay," said Noah. "You know I like to run."

Josh nodded. "I know you're into running. But I need to talk to you. Get in the car, all right?"

Though he didn't want to face more questions, Noah stopped running, went around the car, and climbed in on the passenger side. He might not have done it for anyone else, but Josh had been Noah's best friend since kindergarten. More than once, Noah had thought about telling Josh all about the dreams. But after what had happened with Caroline, he didn't want to take the chance of making Josh think he was totally nuts. He didn't want to lose his best friend.

No sooner had Noah shut the door than Josh slammed the gas pedal to the floor. The Camaro fishtailed down the street, leaving a wash of smoke. Noah buried his fingers in the upholstery as Josh slid the car around a corner and gunned past a stop sign without slowing.

"You trying to break the sound barrier?" Noah asked.

Josh nodded. "I would if I could. Listen, I talked to Coach Harris today."

"What about?"

"About getting you back on the team." Josh's pale gray eyes shifted to Noah for a moment and then turned back to the road. "He never should have suspended you."

Noah choked back a sour laugh. "You've got to be kidding. I missed five practices. And in the last two games I didn't score a point."

"So?" Josh slowed the Camaro just enough to make the turn onto Noah's street. "There's a lot of guys who haven't put it through the hoop all year. You're still the best player on the team. You just had a couple of bad games."

Noah knew it was much worse than a couple of bad games. He had forgotten plays, missed passes, and stumbled around the court like a sick cow. In the second game, he even took a shot at the wrong basket. Noah wasn't happy about it, but he didn't blame the coach for suspending him.

"What did coach say?" Noah asked.

"He said he'd talk to you about it soon," Josh replied.

Noah frowned. "That doesn't sound so good. He probably just wants an excuse to yell at me some more."

"It's not as bad as it sounds." Josh pumped the brakes and brought the car to a stop in front of Noah's house. "I think the Thursday night game really made Coach think. He saw how bad we lost to Central without you there at guard. He's going to let you back on the team. Count on it."

Noah opened his car door. "Thanks." He climbed out, straightened for a moment, then bent to look through the car window. "Don't get yourself in trouble worrying about me, all right?"

"Don't sweat it," Josh replied. Then he paused and remained silent for a moment, staring down at the steering wheel. Finally, he glanced up at Noah. "Hey," he said. "You're feeling better, right?" He reddened and looked down at the steering wheel again. "I mean, I don't want to invade your privacy or anything, but we've been friends for a long time—*best* friends. I don't need to know what happened to you, if you don't want to tell me. But I was worried about you." Josh turned again to look at Noah in the car window, and he smiled wanly. "You *seem* better, anyway."

"Yeah, it's better." Noah wasn't sure if he sounded very convincing. Up until the blackout at the library, he would have said that things *were* getting better. Now he wasn't so sure.

Josh seemed to take Noah at his word. "There you go," he said. "You'll be back in the starting lineup before next Thursday." He gave a quick wave, then steered the Camaro through a U-turn that took it back down the street and away. Even when it was out of sight, Noah could hear the squeal of its wide tires.

Noah turned and trudged up the long walk toward his house. Noah's home was among the largest houses in town, a great stone and brick affair that dominated the neighborhood.

Two decades before, Noah's father had been just another fisherman, trying to eke out a living from the increasingly empty waters off Stone Harbor. But Glenn Templer had gotten lucky. While the rest of the fishermen were struggling to bring in enough crabs and snapper to keep food on the table, Noah's father had sold his boat and invested in obscure high-tech firms. Now he was one of the richest men in town.

No one was home to greet Noah as slipped inside and trotted up the curving staircase. He was glad for that—he wanted the chance to think before he talked to his parents. And he needed the time to work on his project.

The walls of Noah's room were almost completely covered in maps, diagrams, and notes from his project. A trio of state maps were spread across one wall, with dozens of multicolored pins sprayed over their surfaces. On the facing wall, a huge national map was studded with more pins and flagged with stick-on notes. Still more stick-on notes decorated the walls in shades of pink, yellow, and pale blue. On Noah's wide desk, stacks of project notes lay on top of schoolbooks and sports magazines, barely leaving space for Noah's computer.

Noah sat down at his desk and flipped on the computer. Working quickly, he checked the new entries in his notebook against the records already in his project database.

Four of the ten cases turned out to be repeats. The other six were new. As soon as he confirmed that fact, Noah went to the maps behind his bed. Two red pins and two yellow pins served to mark the location of the new cases.

Red pins showed encounters, yellow pins abductions. The rarer green pins were reserved for those cases that seemed the most like Noah's. The placement of all the pins seemed to make no sense, but Noah was convinced it wasn't really random. There was a pattern beginning to form in the little dots of color. Each piece of data added to that pattern. With every pin that went into the map, Noah was one step closer to solving the mystery of what was happening to him.

Just looking at the maps made Noah feel better. He might not be able to do anything about the dreams, and it wasn't anything that he could explain to his friends, but at least he was taking some action. And the map showed that he was not alone. There were other people out there who had suffered something similar. They had survived it, and so would he.

He was getting better. He really was.

Now that the project was taken care of, Noah noticed he was feeling hungry. He bounced up from the end of the bed, pulled a sweatshirt on over his T-shirt, and headed downstairs. He paused at the foot of the stairs.

There were voices coming from the kitchen.

As he walked closer, Noah made out the voices of his mother and father. They were arguing.

That was a surprise in itself. Noah's mother, Margaret Templer, was among the quietest people in the world. Noah could not remember the last time he had heard her raise her voice about anything. But it was raised now, raised loud enough that Noah could make out her words even though he was twenty feet away and on the other side of the closed kitchen door.

"So what?" his mother was saying. "It's not as if we need the scholarship. We have enough money without it."

"That's not the point." Glenn Templer's voice was loud enough to carry the length of the house, but then Noah's father was almost always loud. When he talked, he wanted everyone to listen.

Noah leaned against the cool wood of the kitchen door. He should have known they were arguing about him. Nothing else would have gotten his mother irritated enough to shout.

"Then tell me, what is the point?" said his mother.

"I'm not worried about the basketball team, Marge. I'm worried about Noah. Don't tell me you haven't noticed how he's been acting lately."

For a moment, the kitchen was silent. When Noah's mother started speaking again, her voice was softer, so soft that Noah had to press his ear to the wooden door to hear. "I'll admit that I'm worried, too," replied his mother. "He hasn't gone anywhere with his friends. You know he's not dating Caroline anymore?"

"All he does is sit in his room and doodle on those silly maps," said Noah's father. "I think it's time we called our contact for some help."

Noah pushed himself away from the door and went silently back to the stairs. As quietly as he could, he climbed up the curving staircase, went back to his room, and shut the door.

Things would be fine as soon as the dreams went away. Noah was sure of that, just as he was sure he didn't want to hear what his father had planned for him—although he was probably just going to suggest a psychiatrist. He stared for a solid hour at the pins on his map, wishing for some kind of order that never appeared.

Dee was waiting at the top of the steps when Harley drove her bike into the parking lot the next morning. "You're late," Dee accused cheerfully.

Harley put down the kickstand and propped up the bike. "Only a few minutes," she countered.

"You obviously don't know what kind of people run this school," said Dee. She looked nervously through the door. "Being five minutes tardy is a capital offense."

Dee walked back and forth impatiently as Harley put away her helmet and chained the bike to a signpost. As soon as Harley had reached the top of the stairs, Dee shoved the door open and hurried inside. Harley followed close behind.

The blue-painted corridors of Stone Harbor High were almost deserted. Only a few students were still at their lockers, and those few seemed in a definite hurry.

"Come on," urged Dee. "We've got about ten seconds before we're marked tardy. Two tardies, and you have detention after school for a week."

Harley sighed and shook her head. "I thought once I got away from the military base schools, I'd be free from junk like that."

Dee laughed. "You wait until you get on the wrong side of the principal," she warned. "He thinks this *is* a military base."

28

With Dee leading the way, they skidded into homeroom seconds before the bell sounded. As Harley found a desk and settled in, she caught some glances from the other students. The girls looked at her with flat, appraising expressions. Some of the guys began to whisper to one another. Harley felt like she was on exhibit.

A young woman teacher appeared and started going quickly through the roll. "Kathleen Davisidaro?" called the teacher.

Harley winced. "Harley," she said.

"What?"

"I prefer to be called Harley."

The teacher looked at her oddly. "Harley?"

From the back of the room, one of the guys made a noise like a motorcycle revving up. Laughter rippled through the class.

The teacher scowled and made a note on her list, then carried on with the roll. Harley saw several of the students glancing her way, but whenever she met their eyes, they looked in another direction.

"Not a very friendly bunch," Harley said to Dee as the bell rang and students filed out of the room.

Dee picked up her books and shrugged. "Stone Harbor's kind of a weird place. In the summer we get about a trillion tourists in town. Then fall comes, and it's back to being a little village."

"What's that got to do with being rude?" asked Harley.

"It's the tourist thing," Dee replied. She walked along the hallway as she talked, her books cradled in her arms. "So many people come and go around this place, the townies figure you don't even count until you've been here over the winter. Winter people are real people. Summer people are just an excuse to charge ten bucks for a gallon of milk."

"So I've got to go all year before someone will even talk to me?"

Dee stopped and looked over at Harley. After a moment, she smiled. "No. You're too pretty. The guys will probably hold back for a day or two, just to make it look good. But then they'll be all over you."

Harley scowled. "I'm not pretty."

"Yeah, *right*. I'll see you after last period." Dee gave a quick wave and disappeared down the crowded hall.

During the rest of day, Harley had little time to think about anything but schoolwork. As usual after changing schools, she found that she was ahead in some classes, way behind in others. By the time her final class began, Harley felt as though she had run a marathon. She slumped down in a chair in the back of the classroom, staring blankly at the caricatures of famous writers over the blackboard. Her head was aching at the thought of all the studying to come.

While Harley was sitting there worrying, a tall figure settled into the chair in front of her. Harley looked up and saw that it was Noah Templer. With his long legs wedged under the desk, Noah looked something like an adult sitting in a first-grade class-room—a *cute* adult. Despite what Dee had said, Noah didn't look crazy. Harley realized that something *felt* wrong about him, though. Noah was doing nothing but sitting there, but she sensed a crackling field of tension all around him. Harley wished he would turn around so she could see the expression in Noah's deep blue eyes.

Harley opened her mouth to talk to Noah, but before she could think of anything to say, the bell rang to signal the start of English class. Once again Harley found herself taking pages of notes. Halfway through class, she looked up and saw that Noah was also working in his notebook. Harley leaned forward in her seat to peer over his shoulder.

Noah wasn't taking notes—he was drawing. Though Harley couldn't see all of what Noah was sketching on his pad, she could see enough. Over and over he had drawn an oval shape. To each oval he'd added two smaller dark ovals, forming a simple face. But there was something wrong with those faces. They were too long, and the eyes were far too large. Maybe Noah was drawing someone wearing a weird helmet. Maybe they weren't faces at all. At least not of *people*. A gentle shiver trailed down Harley's arms. Something about Noah's drawings seemed naggingly familiar.

Abruptly, Noah stiffened. Harley looked away, sure that he knew she was watching him. When she dared to peek again, Noah had flipped over a clean sheet of paper and was filling it with lines of tiny letters Harley couldn't make out.

Harley slumped back into her chair. Whatever Noah was doing, it had nothing to do with English class, she was sure of that much. Maybe Dee was right. Maybe Noah was . . . what was the word Dee had used? *Bonkaroonie,* Harley recalled with a smile.

When the bell rang to signal the end of the school day, Noah was up from his chair and out the door before Harley could even gather her books. She got out to the hallway just in time to see him hurrying away, his blond hair bobbing above the crowd of shorter students.

Dee emerged from the throng. "Well," she asked, "did you survive your first day in Fun Land, USA?"

Harley nodded, still watching Noah. "I guess. It's going to take me months to catch up, though. You guys are way ahead of me."

"Yeah, we're all brainiacs around here." Dee nodded toward a knot of cheerleaders talking at the other end of the hall. "Take that group. I think they're all up for a Nobel Prize." She tapped a finger against her chin as if she were thinking hard. "Chemistry, I think. Or maybe it was the Nobel Prize . . . for eyeliner."

Harley couldn't stop herself from laughing. "So what would you do if I wanted to go out for cheerleader?"

Dee stared at her in horror. "I'd only be devastated. Though it would be fun to see Caroline Crewson scrambling to hold her spot."

"Don't worry," Harley assured her new friend. "I've never had the coordination to do anything like cheerleading without falling flat on my face. Besides, I'm in no hurry to bounce up and down in front of a thousand people." She looked down the hallway. "I *would* like to try out for the track team. That is, if you even *have* a girls' track team."

"Sure," said Dee. "We're not *complete* barbarians. Follow me."

Dee led the way through the school and across an empty playground to a huge old gym perched at the top of a small hill. Harley could see runners appearing and disappearing behind the building as they moved around the oval of a track.

"Coach Rocklin!" shouted Dee.

A woman at the side of the track looked up. Even from a distance, Harley could see the coach wince and roll her eyes.

"Looks like you're really great pals with the coach," Harley observed.

Dee nodded. "We have a deal. She doesn't make me run, she doesn't have to listen to me whine about running. Come on. I'll introduce you."

Coach Rocklin was a short woman, no taller than Dee. But she was as lean as a greyhound. From the look of her, Harley guessed that the coach could outrun most of the team.

"I don't suppose you've come down to actually *volunteer* for anything, Janes," the coach said.

"Not a chance," Dee replied. She stopped beside the coach and nodded toward Harley. "Here's your new victim. She says she's interested in the track team."

"Is she?" Coach Rocklin looked Harley up and down. "New student?"

Harley nodded. "Harley Davisidaro. I just moved here from California, and—"

"Now if you'll excuse me," Dee interrupted, "I'm going to go watch the guys run." She wandered off across the field.

The coach glanced around to check that the runners

were still working, then turned her attention back to Harley. "Have you done some running?"

"I was on the team at my last school."

"And are you any good?"

Harley shrugged. "I won some races."

"What distance?"

"Middle distance," Harley answered. "Mostly the mile and the fifteen hundred."

Coach Rocklin winced. "Middle distance. I'm afraid I've already got enough milers to form a line a mile long."

Harley's stomach knotted with disappointment. Although she had been moved to a dozen different schools, she had always been on the track team. It was the one thing she could hold on to. "Can I try out? Maybe I can win a spot."

"Well . . ." The coach pursed her lips for a second, then shook her head firmly. "This is my first year at this school, but some of these girls have been working together for years. I'm not ready to toss anyone off the team."

Harley didn't want to sound upset in front of the coach, but she couldn't disguise the disappointment in her voice. "So I'm not even going to get a chance?"

The coach's expression softened. "You'll get a chance. How about right now? Do a lap for me."

"But I've got jeans on," Harley protested.

"I'm not asking you to set a record," the coach replied. "Just let me see that you can run. Take it easy."

Harley nodded. "Okay." She dropped her backpack on the grass at the side of the track and stretched for a few moments. Then she started off around the track.

As soon as she started running, Harley felt better. It took a few steps for her stride to loosen, and her jeans kept her from going all out, but halfway around the track she had forgotten all about how much English homework was waiting for her. Instead, she felt the air moving in and out of her lungs, her legs pistoning against the ground, and her hair streaming out in the wind. As she rounded the last turn of the oval, Harley caught up to a trio of runners. It was a mixed group, two girls and one guy. As Harley began to move past them, their heads turned slightly in her direction. The guy at the front of the group was thin and tall, with short blond hair so pale it was almost white. He lengthened his stride as Harley drew near, moving away from the others. Harley matched him.

Down the straight, they increased the pace. With every step Harley was an inch closer to the leader. She had the wonderful feeling that she'd experienced only from serious running—the feeling that she wasn't moving herself so much as rolling the world under her feet. Only ten yards from the end of the straight, she pulled ahead of the other runner.

Harley struggled to a stop next to Coach Rocklin. She was breathing hard, but not really panting. Under her heavy clothing, sweat rolled down her skin. The lap had only been enough to get Harley warmed up. She wished she had brought her gear. She really wanted to go back out there and run a couple of miles.

"Very nice," the coach remarked. "But I said take

it easy. You shouldn't have pushed yourself so hard without warming up."

"That *was* warming up," Harley replied. She pulled in a deep breath and smiled. "Next time I'll *really* run."

The coach snorted. "I like confidence," she said. "And I like what I see in you."

"So you're going to let me run middle distance?"

"No," the coach answered. "At least not right now. I want you to think about the longer races. I've got a real need for someone at the 10K length."

The thought of running a race that long made Harley wince. But it was obviously the best deal she was going to get. "I'll try it," she accepted. "What do I do now?"

"Come here after school tomorrow," Rocklin instructed. "Be ready to run." The coach held out her hand. "Welcome to the team."

Harley shook the coach's hand. "Thanks."

Rocklin nodded. "No problem. Now, if you'll excuse me, I need to go get the sprinters back in gear." She shoved her whistle between her lips and blew a short blast. Then she marched off across the track.

Harley pushed her hair back from her face and watched the other runners go around the track. Now, even if she never became popular at Stone Harbor High, she would always have a place where she belonged. Between Dee and the track team, it was turning out to be a pretty good day.

"You looked good out there," a voice said.

When she turned, Harley found Noah Templer standing close behind her. Instead of the clothes he had worn in class, he was now dressed in a gray T-shirt and matching running shorts.

"Thanks," Harley said. She couldn't help admiring his long, muscular legs.

"I'm Noah Templer," Noah said. He grinned crookedly. "I promise not to run over you today."

Harley smiled back. "My name's Harley. And from now on, I'll know to stay out of your way."

"Hmm," Noah said. "I don't think I like that idea. So, are you going to be on the track team?"

"I guess," Harley replied. "Are you on the team?"

Noah shrugged. "Sometimes."

His short answer left Harley searching for something interesting to say. It had been years since any guy had made her feel so awkward. They stood there smiling at each other for a long moment.

"Anyway," Noah said finally, breaking the silence. He pointed at Harley's feet. "Did you know you're overstriding?"

Harley blinked. "Over*what*ing?"

"Overstriding," he repeated. "Your stride is so long that you're losing some of the power. You need to cut back a little."

"But . . . you said yourself I'm running well," Harley said.

"You can run better," Noah replied. "I . . ." He stopped, swallowed, and looked away.

"What's wrong?" Harley asked, alarmed at the ashen color of his face.

"Nothing." Noah shook his head, and his usual healthy coloring returned to his cheeks. "I mean, why don't you meet me after practice tomorrow? You said you liked to run. Maybe we could run together."

Harley felt a burst of confused emotions. She thought Noah was really attractive, but there was no denying that there was something strange about him. Still, it was just running. It wasn't a real date. "Sure," she said after a moment. "I'll see you then."

Noah opened his mouth as if he were going to say something more, but then he nodded and walked away. Seconds later he was making laps on the track, his long legs eating up the distance.

Dee came back from the other side of the oval. "You get things worked out with Coach Rocklin?"

"I think so," Harley replied.

Dee pointed across the field. "What about Noah? I saw you talking to him."

Harley turned to watch Noah make another lap around the track. "He says he can help me with my running."

"Maybe he can," Dee said. "Noah's pretty fast. Whenever they can get him to run he usually wins."

"Yeah. We're going to get together tomorrow."

"You are?" Dee clutched at her heart. "Oh no!"

Harley frowned. "What? You think I shouldn't?"

Dee shook her head. "No. I just wanted Noah for myself."

"But you even said he was nuts."

"He is, but I don't let little things like that bother me." Dee looked around at Noah and frowned. "Noah and I used to talk all the time, even after we stopped going out," she said. "Now he never calls. . . ." For the first time, there was no hint of a joke in Dee's voice.

Harley laid a hand lightly on the smaller girl's shoulder. "Maybe I shouldn't go with him tomorrow."

Dee shook her head. "No, you should go. I *think* . . ." She stopped and shrugged. "Come on. I'll let you give me a ride home." She turned and started down the hill beside the gym.

"Wow," said Harley. "What a privilege."

"Hey," said Dee. "What are friends for?" She led the way to Harley's motorcycle.

As Harley turned to follow, she caught sight of a tall figure at the other side of the track. It was the boy she had beaten in her run, the one with the pale hair. He was staring directly at her.

Harley swallowed hard. Even from a hundred yards away, she could feel the intensity of his glare. She shivered and turned away. But all the way down the hill, she could still feel his gaze boring into her back.

Harley would have sworn those eyes held pure hate.

At first, the shapes were nothing but a vague white mass floating in the eerie empty room, like a cluster of light bulbs seen through dense fog. Slowly they grew larger and clearer. They were faces. Their mouths were only a thin, lipless line. There was no sign of a nose. But they were faces, faces dominated by huge, solid black eyes. Dead eyes. Eyes as flat and empty as those of a shark.

Noah wanted to scream. He wanted to hit those white faces, or run, or do anything to get out of that place. But he did nothing. His body was as frozen as the heart of winter. He couldn't even blink.

The glowing faces circled around him slowly, like a model of the solar system spinning around the sun. Or wolves circling around their prey. Long glowing fingers drifted out to touch, then pulled back. There was a constant low hum—a babble of voices speaking softly in an unknown language. Beyond the faces, the room was as dark as soot.

Suddenly, a new face leered out of the darkness. A human face.

"This won't take long," said a cold, emotionless voice. There was a glint of something slender and metallic. A knife. Or maybe a scalpel. It moved so fast it was hard to see. The blade flashed down.

The voice spoke again, but now the words were fuzzy, unclear. Everything in the room grew blurry and dim.

Then everything snapped back to razor-sharp clarity. "Almost done now," said the voice. The blade came down in a silvery arc, whistling through the air like a falling bomb.

Noah screamed. He reached out, beating his hands against the air.

The faces were gone.

Noah's breath came in strangled gasps. He was in his own room, in his own bed, not in some strange empty place. In the dim light that spilled under his door from the hallway, Noah could make out the square shapes of his heavy wooden furniture. He could see the glowing numbers on his alarm clock. There were no faces. No scalpel. It was another dream.

Knuckles rapped against his bedroom door. "Noah?" his father asked. "Noah, are you all right?"

Noah tried to answer, but at first nothing came from his mouth but a kind of faint, wordless moan. He took a deep breath, swallowed hard, and tried again.

"Yeah, Dad," he called. "I'm okay."

The door creaked open a couple of inches, and Noah saw his father silhouetted against the light from the hallway. Unlike Noah, his father was short and broad as a bear. His wide figure filled the door frame. No one ever would have guessed that Mr. Templer and Noah were father and son. "You sure?"

"Yeah. I'm fine." The truth was that Noah's heart was hammering against his chest so hard, it was a wonder his ribs didn't break.

His father hesitated for a moment. Then he nodded

and closed the door. Noah heard the floorboards creak as he moved away down the hall.

After a few minutes of lying awake in the bed, Noah sat up and swung his feet down to touch the cold wooden floor. There would be no more sleep tonight. He knew from experience that once the dreams had come, sleep was impossible.

He stood in the dimly lit room, staring at the tiny pins on his maps. There were other people out there who had the same problem. He was not alone. Noah sat down at the computer and logged on to the Internet, searching for more cases.

By the time the sun came up, Noah felt in control again. The smell of bacon from downstairs let him know that his parents were up and about. It was getting close to time for school. He logged off the computer and started to get dressed for the day.

Noah yawned as he pulled his shirt over his head. This was the third time that the dreams had woken him in the middle of the night. He was getting too tired to be nervous. He wished the dreams would leave him alone long enough to get a good night's sleep.

Breakfast slipped past without a mention of Noah's behavior, but he could feel the tension from his parents' unasked questions. Afterward Noah packed his school clothes in his backpack and dressed in his sweats. He yawned again as he was getting ready. He was so tired, he almost felt like driving. If he hadn't remembered that he was supposed to meet Harley, he might have given in to the desire to take his car.

The school was dark when Noah arrived. He unlocked the door at the side of the athletics building and slipped into the cavernous, empty gym. The squeak of Noah's running shoes on the hardwood floor echoed through the shadowed space as he crossed the basketball court and trotted down the stairs into the boys' locker room.

The gym was over fifty years old. Renovation and repair kept it looking pretty good up where the spectators sat. Down in the locker rooms, it showed its age. The floor in the boys' locker room was cracked, pitted concrete covered only by a worn coat of gray paint. The lockers were broken and rusty, with initials of long-gone students carved in their doors. The showers put out a reluctant stream of icy cold water. The locker room was by far the barest, coldest, ugliest place in the school—and it had always been one of Noah's favorite places in the world.

Taking his morning shower at the school each day made Noah feel like he was roughing it. When the locker room was filled with guys after a basketball game, it was full of motion and color. When he was there by himself, it was like taking a daily expedition to some secret, silent place, like an archaeologist discovering a lost ancient ruin.

Noah undressed quickly. The handle on the faucet squeaked as he turned on the shower. Shivering in the cold water, he worked to clean off the sweat from his morning run.

He was almost done with his shower when a flicker of movement caught his eye.

Noah froze. He blinked soapy water out of his eyes and peered into the locker room. He cranked the water down until it dribbled to a stop. The feeling that someone was watching him had returned.

Nothing moved. There was no one else in the locker room.

Noah was about to turn the water back on when he heard a noise. It was faint, but Noah had definitely heard something. A shadow moved by the door. Someone was just outside the locker room.

This time, it was no dream. Someone really *was* watching him.

Moving as quietly as he could, Noah left the shower. Still dripping wet, he pulled on his sweatpants. Then he crept barefoot toward the door.

Before he could get there, the faint sound outside turned into the thud of feet running away. Noah sprinted out of the locker room and up the steps to the basketball court. As he topped the stairs, he ran head-on into a large, solid figure.

With a grunt, the figure fell to the floor. Noah reached down and grabbed the intruder by the front of his shirt. Now he was finally going to get some answers. He pulled the figure up, and found himself staring face-to-face with Josh McQuinn.

"Gee, Templer," Josh said. "You always this grumpy in the morning?"

Noah stared at his friend in surprise. "Josh? What were you doing down there?"

"Down where?"

"The locker room."

Josh shook his head. "I wasn't anywhere near the locker room. I just came in. Now, how about letting me go?"

With his hands still balled in Josh's shirt, Noah looked quickly around the gym. The space seemed as empty as it had been when he came in. "You see anyone else in here?" Noah asked.

"You mean besides the soaking wet psychopath that knocked me down?" Josh shook his head. "Nobody's here. Now let me go, all right?"

Embarrassed, Noah released his hold on his friend. "Sorry," he said. "I was taking a shower, and I was sure someone was looking in at me."

"Yeah, well," Josh replied. "It wasn't me." He dabbed at a thin line of blood that ran down from the corner of his mouth where Noah's head had smashed against Josh's lip. "It wasn't me. I'm not into that kind of thing."

A sliver of doubt ran through Noah. He hadn't actually seen anyone. "I was sure that someone was there," he said.

"Maybe," said Josh. "But I didn't see anybody." He looked at Noah and frowned. "If I was you, I'd get back into the shower before Coach Harris saw me dripping water on his basketball court."

Noah realized that he was standing there soaking wet, with his hair still full of soap. "Hang on," he said. "I'll be back in a second."

He ran back to the locker room and rinsed off quickly. Then he dried himself and slipped into his school clothes. When he returned to the gym, he found Josh waiting for him on one of the old wooden bleachers.

"You plan on knocking me down again?" asked Josh. He held up his hands like a boxer. "Maybe you want to punch me first?"

"Sorry," Noah said again. "I really thought there was someone spying on me."

Josh shrugged and dropped his hands. "Next time I'll whistle so you know I'm coming."

"What are you doing over here before school, anyway?"

"Looking for you," Josh answered. "I figured this was the best place to catch you."

"What's up now?" asked Noah. "Coach say anything more about letting me back on the team?"

Josh shook his head. "No. I was just coming to see if you wanted to meet me here after school and do a little one-on-one."

"You think we can put it off till tomorrow?" Noah asked. "I've kind of got plans today."

"What kind of plans?"

"Nothing, really," Noah replied. For some reason, he didn't feel like telling Josh who he was going to meet. "Just going to do some running."

Josh snorted. "You run every day. Blow it off for today and shoot some hoops instead."

Noah ran his fingers through his damp hair. "I would . . . ," he said slowly, realizing that he was going to have to explain. "But I sort of agreed to meet someone."

"Yeah?" Josh raised an eyebrow in interest. "You and Caroline going somewhere?"

"No, I'm going running with Harley Davisidaro."

"The new girl?" Josh's thin face turned down in a frown.

"What's the matter?" Noah asked. "You're not interested in her, are you?"

"No, no!" Josh replied quickly. "It's just that—"

"What?" Noah's voice came out more sharply than he'd intended.

"Nothing," Josh finished lamely. "She just seems like bad news to me, that's all."

A distant bell sounded, warning that the start of the school day was near. "Yeah, well . . . we'd better go," Noah said quickly. He and Josh hurried out of the gym, with Noah striding a pace ahead to prevent Josh from saying anything else about Harley.

Several times during the day, Noah thought about her. When she sat down behind him in English class, Noah found himself getting unexpectedly nervous. He took every excuse he could to turn in his seat and take a glance at Harley.

Her long black hair had been pulled back in a loose heavy mass. She didn't wear lots of makeup or jewelry like so many of the other girls at school. Maybe her nose was a little too long to be called cute. Maybe her jaw was a little too strong. None of that kept him from deciding that Harley was gorgeous.

Throughout track practice, as Noah did his laps around the track, he continued to steal glances at her. It didn't look like she was having a lot of fun. Coach Rocklin spent a lot of the practice just talking to Harley, or making Harley run back and forth on the strip in front of her. By the time practice ended, it was obvious that Harley was frustrated.

Noah slowed his pace around the track and jogged over to Harley's side. "Hi," he said. "Feel like you're ready to race?"

Harley shook her head. "I'm not sure I ever will be. Coach says the same thing about my running that you did." She looked down at her feet and frowned. "I've been on nearly a dozen track teams, and this is the first time anyone ever said there was something wrong with the way I was running."

"You're fast," Noah told her. "When you win races, people let you alone. But Coach Rocklin is good. She wants you to do the best you can."

"I don't know," Harley replied doubtfully. "I feel like I'm about to fall over my own feet."

Noah gave what he hoped was a reassuring smile. "You'll get used to it. You ready to run with me? Since Coach Rocklin has already beat you up, we can just take it easy."

Harley nodded. "Yeah, I need to run. Where are we going?"

"I thought we'd do about four miles out and back," said Noah. "If you'll go that far with me, I'll show you another Stone Harbor."

Harley looked puzzled. "Another Stone Harbor?"

"You'll see."

Noah ran out of the school yard, keeping his pace easy as he traveled down the sidewalk next to the school. Harley fell in at his side, her smooth, tan legs matching Noah's stride for stride. For the first time since the dreams had started, Noah lost the creepy feeling that someone was following him.

"Have you had much of a chance to look around?" Noah asked after a few minutes.

"Not yet. I . . ." Harley stopped talking for a moment and caught her breath. "I haven't seen anything but the main road. And the way to Dee's house."

"I'm glad you met Dee," said Noah. "She's great."

Harley glanced up at him for a moment, then nodded. "She likes you a lot."

Noah could hear the insinuation in her voice, and his back stiffened slightly as he ran. "Dee and I are only friends," he told Harley.

"I'm not so sure Dee wants it that way," Harley said softly.

Noah thought about that for a block or two. Dee was easy to talk to, and he enjoyed being with her, but there was a spark missing. Dee would always be just a friend. "Dee has to get over that," he said as they reached the edge of the business district. "Besides, you and I are only running together. It's not like I've asked you to the fall dance."

"I guess not," Harley replied with a shrug.

They ran on through the center of Stone Harbor, dodging around slower pedestrians on the sidewalks. As they passed the grocery store and neared the center of town, Noah suddenly realized that he hadn't thought about the dreams for the whole afternoon.

Noah looked over at Harley and watched her run for a few strides. He liked the way her hair bounced as she ran. More than that, he liked the way she had taken his thoughts away from the dreams. "So," he said. "Want to go to the dance?"

Harley coughed, choked, and staggered to a stop. "You're not serious," she said in a strained voice.

"I'm not sure," Noah replied. He smiled at her. "But I think I am. Yeah, I know I am."

Harley pushed a wisp of stray black hair away from her face. "Maybe we should wait until we've at least had a real date?"

"Okay," said Noah. "But . . ." He stopped in the middle of his sentence, staring into the window on the other side of Harley.

Inside the old grocery store, a butcher was working on a large cut of beef. The knife went up and down, up and down, sawing through the flesh.

As the knife moved, it seemed to cut Noah free of the street around him. The sound of passing cars faded into the distance. The sunlight dimmed.

"Get prepared," a cold voice intoned.

The butcher raised his knife. . . .

"The insertion will be simple."

The knife came down, and . . .

"Get ready to test reception."

The knife came up . . .

"This subject looks very promising."

The knife came down . . .

"We'll need to expand our data channels."

The knife came up . . .

The street around Noah was completely gone now. He was back in the dark room, lying frozen on a table of cold metal, surrounded by glowing black-eyed faces. A human figure leaned over him, a slim gleaming scalpel in its hand.

"Almost done now," said the cold voice.

For the first time, Noah recognized that voice, and he recognized the face that stared down at him from the darkness.

It was his best friend. Josh McQuinn.

Harley reached out and touched Noah softly on the arm. "Are you all right?" she asked.

Noah swayed on his feet. "Almost done now," he said. His voice was distant, as if he were talking from the bottom of a well. Though he was looking toward Harley, his eyes seemed to be focused on something far in the distance.

"Almost done with what?" Harley asked. "Noah, are you sure you're all right?"

"The trans-alpha patterns are coming through," Noah said. His face was slack and pale.

"Noah!" Harley said more loudly. "Noah, what's wrong?" She took him by the arm and shook him.

Suddenly Noah jerked. He looked at Harley, then spun back and forth looking up and down the street.

Harley released her grip on his arm. "Are you all right?"

Noah turned back to her. His cheeks were flushed and his eyes were wild. "I just remembered something," he said. His voice was little more than a whisper.

"What?"

"Something from a dream." Noah blinked and shook his head rapidly. "I'm all right now," he said.

Harley let out a long breath. "You scared me," she said. "Do you need to go home? Or maybe you should see a doctor."

"No." Noah looked at Harley. His blue eyes were

full of an emotion she didn't understand. "Will you stay with me?"

The sudden change in Noah had frightened Harley. One moment he had seemed so normal. The next he had frozen and stared off like a zombie. Even though Dee had said Noah was nuts, Harley hadn't really believed it. Now she was beginning to wonder.

"What do you want to do?" she asked carefully.

"Let's just run," Noah said. "I think I need to run."

"Sure," Harley replied. "If that's what you want."

Noah charged off down the street at a pace much faster than they had been running before. Harley had to open up and run hard just to keep up with him. She shifted her eyes to the side, watching Noah as he ran. She was afraid that any moment he might start acting strange again.

But Noah only ran harder. There was no more talk now, no jokes about dances. Harley needed all her breath just to keep up the pace.

They passed through several subdivisions of neat brick homes and headed down a gentle slope. A cool breeze came up the slope, bringing with it the smell of the ocean. Finally, they cleared a last line of trees and the Atlantic Ocean was revealed, spread out ahead of them.

Noah stopped. "This is what I wanted to show you," he said.

The ocean was a deep, grayish blue, rolling with swells and laced with thin ribbons of white foam. The beach was pale brown sand interrupted by nothing but a few small dunes and stands of yellow saw grass.

A hundred yards back from the edge of the water, a highway ran parallel to the beachfront. All along the highway were town houses, condos, beach homes, and businesses. Off to the right, the twisting frame of a roller coaster stood in the middle of a small amusement park.

"Wow," Harley said once she caught her breath. "You were right. It really *is* like another town."

"This is the summer town," Noah told her. "When the tourists are here, all these stands are open and everything down here is busy. But as soon as they're gone, it all shuts down."

Noah jogged down the rest of the slope at a much more gentle pace. He ran across the highway and led the way onto a long wooden pier. Harley followed him out to the end of the pier and stood with him at the railing. Below them, the ocean slapped against wooden pilings. Seagulls flew overhead, spinning and hovering in the sea breeze.

"It's gorgeous out here," Harley said, taking a deep breath of the salty, delicious ocean air.

Noah nodded. "I like to come out to this pier. It's been here a long time." He ran his hand along the wooden railing. "My father used to run a fishing boat right off this same pier. My grandfather, too." He turned to her and grinned. "Want to know something kind of funny?" he asked. "I'm the first person in my whole family to get seasick—and I mean for generations. Isn't that weird?"

Harley leaned against the railing and returned his smile. She looked into Noah's eyes and saw that the strange distant expression was gone. But that didn't mean it wouldn't come back. It occurred to her that they were a long way away from the school, and that no one else knew where they were. If Noah did anything else strange, she was on her own.

"Are you ready to go back?" Harley asked. She was tired from the run, and getting to the school—where there were other people around—seemed like a good idea.

"No, not yet," said Noah. He hesitated for a moment, then gently put his hand on Harley's arm. "I want to explain what happened back in town."

Harley bit her lip and looked down at Noah's hand. "You don't have to say anything."

"Yes, I do," Noah replied. He took his hand away and turned to face the rolling sea. "If I don't tell you, you're going to think I'm crazy."

Harley wasn't sure there was anything he could say that would make a difference, but she nodded in agreement. "All right. What happened?"

"Like I said," Noah replied, "I remembered something."

"It must have been something important."

"I don't know yet," Noah answered distractedly. "Maybe it was." He stopped for a moment and drew in a deep breath. "Listen," he said. "I've only told one person what's really going on with me, and she thought I was nuts. For some reason, I have a feeling you'll take me seriously."

Before Noah could continue, there was the sound of a car door slamming at the end of the pier. Harley looked back toward the road and saw a dark green sedan with the letters THRF on the side surrounded by an upward-pointing triangle. The passenger door opened, and a man climbed out.

For a moment, Harley thought it might be her father, but as he started down the pier, she realized it was one of the guards from the research base. The one who had carried the clipboard.

The guard walked rapidly down the pier. Even from fifty feet away, Harley could hear the man's boot heels clapping on the boards like gunshots with each step.

"What's going on?" asked Noah. "Who's this guy?"

Harley shook her head. "He's from the base where my dad works," she replied. "But I don't know what he's doing here."

Clipboard marched up and stopped ten feet away from Harley. "Ms. Davisidaro," he said. "You were difficult to locate."

"I'll bet," Harley said. "Why did you want to find me, anyway?"

"That question will be answered when you return to the base," said the guard. "Come with me." He turned and started back down the pier.

"Wait!" Harley called. "Is something wrong with my dad?"

The guard spoke without turning. "The commander will answer your questions at the base."

A touch on her arm made Harley jump. She spun around and saw Noah looking at her with concern.

"What should I do?" he asked.

"I don't know." There was a cold lump of fear in Harley's stomach. It had to be her father.

"Are you going to go with him?" asked Noah.

Harley nodded. "I guess so. I need to find out what's going on."

"Do you want me to come with you?"

"No. No, I don't think so." Harley turned to Noah and gave him the closest thing she could manage to a smile. "I'll be all right."

Noah frowned, but after a moment he nodded. "Okay. If you need anything, just give me a call."

Harley nodded. She reached out quickly and took Noah's hand. "I'll see you at school tomorrow." She gave his hand a squeeze, then ran after the guard.

The guard reached the car and got in stiffly. The back door to the car swung open as Harley approached. She climbed inside.

The driver of the car was a woman with short brown hair and a faint pink scar along her cheek. She wore the same dark undecorated uniform as the other guard.

"What's wrong?" Harley asked again. Neither guard replied to her question as the car pulled away from the pier and headed along the coast road.

"We need to go by the school," said Harley. "I left my bike there. My clothes and my pass card are there, too."

"We have those already," Clipboard told her. "We'll give them back to you when we get to the base."

Harley gritted her teeth at the thought of someone else riding her bike. She sat in the backseat and watched Stone Harbor go past. She wished the woman would drive faster. The fear that had started in Harley's stomach was spreading. In her mind, she played out the possible things that might have happened.

Her father was an expert in electronics. Harley wasn't sure just what it was he was working on, but electronics had to mean electricity. Maybe her father had been shocked in an accident. Maybe he had been killed. Just the thought was enough to start Harley's heart beating far faster than it had during her run.

Finally the sedan rolled up to the gate, and they were waved into the base. They drove past the house where Harley and her father had been living for the last few days and pulled up at a cluster of small, gray, blocky buildings.

"The commander is waiting for you inside," Clipboard told Harley. He made no move to get out of the car himself.

Harley climbed out and walked to the nearest building, her heart pounding in her throat as she stepped inside. There was no secretary. The front room was nothing but a bare table surrounded by twin rows of chairs. Beyond that, a single door was marked with a large brass plaque that read Col. M. Braddock.

Harley walked over to the door and knocked. "Hello?"

The door swung open so quickly that Harley jumped back. On the other side was a stocky man with a thin mustache and graying hair that had receded to leave a bald patch at the crown of his head. Like the guards, he wore a solid blue uniform with absolutely no ribbons or medals.

"You must be Kathleen!" he called cheerfully.

Harley wasn't sure where Colonel Braddock was from, but there was a strange lilting accent to his voice. He smiled broadly. His eyes were the same dark gray as his hair.

Harley swallowed. "Are you the commander?"

"That's right." The stocky man held out his hand. "Martin Braddock." His handshake was firm and dry. "You're not in the unit, so you're welcome to call me Martin."

"You . . . you wanted to see me?" asked Harley. Braddock was acting far friendlier than Harley had expected. It only made her more nervous.

"Yes, yes." The base commander stepped back from the doorway. "Come on in here. Have a seat."

The office beyond the door was as lavish as the room outside was bare. Patterned Oriental carpets were flung on the floor. Cherry wood bookshelves ran from floor to ceiling, with every inch of space crammed with old volumes bound in leather. There was a desk topped with polished black onyx, and a pair of tall chairs. The air-conditioning was set so cold that Harley shivered as the air blew across her arms.

Braddock walked around behind the gleaming desk and dropped into a chair. "I'm so glad to see they found you," he said. "I was afraid you might be worried if you got back here before we could explain what happened."

"What's going on?" asked Harley. "Is my father okay?"

"Of course he is." The commander flashed another smile. "Now please, sit down." His words were polite, but the way he spoke made it clear he expected Harley to obey.

Harley sat. The leather chair was cold against her bare legs. "If my father's not hurt, then why am I here?"

Instead of answering right away, Braddock pulled open a drawer and drew out a slim manila folder. He placed it on top of the desk and flipped through a few pages. "Your father's in fine health, but this meeting does concern him."

Fear jabbed at Harley again. "What's wrong?"

"Nothing's wrong," said the commander. "It's just that your father was assigned to a rather sensitive project today. A project that will require him to be away for some time."

Harley felt a profound sense of relief that her father was okay—followed by a feeling of disappointment that she would be left alone. "When is he leaving?" she asked.

The commander shuffled around more papers. "I'm afraid he's already gone."

Harley frowned. "He left without saying goodbye?" In all the years that her father had been working on government contracts, he had never done anything like this.

"We didn't give him much choice," said the commander. "He was needed in place today. We operated within the limits of the contract that your father signed."

Harley sat up straight in the leather chair. "Where is he? How long will he be gone?"

Braddock sighed. "Those are questions I'm afraid

I can't answer. His location is top secret. The assignment may take only a matter of days. It may take longer. With that in mind, we've already contacted your aunt Elizabeth."

A wave of confusion swept over Harley. "Aunt Elizabeth? Why did you call *her?*"

"Well," said Braddock, "you'll need to stay somewhere while your father's away. We contacted your aunt at your father's recommendation."

The spark of doubt that had been growing in Harley burst into a roaring flame. "But my father doesn't even *talk* to his sister. I haven't seen her since I was five years old."

Braddock cleared his throat and looked down at the folder. "Your aunt is quite anxious to see you. She has agreed that you should come and stay with her." The commander produced a sheet of paper and slid it across the desk. "We've made the arrangements for you to go to her this evening."

Harley glanced down at the page and saw the details of a plane reservation that would take her to LA. She hadn't even known her aunt was living in LA. Harley felt as if she had been hit on the head with a rock. Her father was gone. She was expected to leave town in a matter of hours. The office seemed to sway around her. Then anger boiled up to replace her confusion.

"No," she said firmly.

"No?" The commander looked puzzled. "What do you mean?"

"I mean *no,*" Harley replied. She stood up. "Look, my dad and I have taken care of each other ever since my mom died. We're a team. I'm not going to go crawling to his sister just because he's out of town for a few days."

"It could be longer," the commander said quickly.

"And it might not," added Harley. "You said yourself that you didn't know." She shook her head. "I'm going to stay here and wait for Dad."

In an instant, the commander's expression turned icy cold. "I'm not prepared to care for an unsupervised child on my base," he said.

"I'm *seventeen,* not seven," Harley shot back. "I'm not a child." She crossed her arms. "I'm staying here."

The commander snatched back the airline reservation and shoved it roughly into the folder. "I see," he said. Braddock drew in a breath that hissed between his teeth. "I will remind you that seventeen is not legally an adult. If you choose to remain here, you will do so under my direct supervision."

Harley didn't particularly like the sound of that, but she nodded. "All right. You let me stay here, and you won't have any trouble."

"We'll see," said the commander. "In any case, should your father be delayed more than a few days, I will reevaluate this situation." His gray eyes gleamed like steel.

Harley nodded, stood up, and walked out of the office. She closed Braddock's door, then paused in the outer office and leaned against the long table.

This was all wrong.

Her father was an electronics expert, not some kind of spy. He didn't go on secret missions, and he didn't run off without letting Harley know he was leaving. There was something more going on here, something that no one wanted to talk about.

Harley sniffed. Tears started to well up in her eyes, but she rubbed them away angrily and marched out to the car.

She was not going let the guards see how upset she was. She was going to go home and wait for her father. And if he didn't show up soon, she would find him herself.

By the time Noah got back to the school, it was almost dark. The trees in front of the school towered against the violet sky and cast long tangled shadows across the campus. The school itself was as dark and quiet as some ancient ruin.

He worried about the strange car that had come to pick up Harley. He had heard that her father worked out of the little military base south of town. But it was hard for Noah to think of a reason why people from the base would be coming to get Harley. At least, it was hard to think of a *good* reason.

As he turned the corner and ran down to the gym, Noah noticed that Harley's motorcycle was gone. The only car that remained in the parking lot was Josh McQuinn's red Camaro.

Seeing Josh's car made Noah stumble to a stop. In all the dreams, there was always one human face among all the bloated, glowing forms. Until today, Noah had never been able to identify that face. Now he knew it was Josh's.

Which made absolutely no sense at all.

Not only had Noah been friends with Josh since they were kids, there was no way Josh could do the things the person in the dream was doing. Josh was just a high-school student, not some kind of mad doctor. The idea of him cutting on Noah in some bizarre operation was too ridiculous to even consider.

In a strange way, putting Josh's face together with the dreams made Noah feel better. The whole thing was so silly, it only served to prove that the dreams were just what they seemed—dreams, and nothing more.

Noah went down to the locker room and collected his things. He looked for Josh in the gym, but there was no sign of anyone else in the building. When Noah came back upstairs and left the gym, Josh's car was gone.

He was ten steps out the door when he noticed that the world around him was fading to gray. A murmur of strange voices rose in his ears. Pale faces rose up on the edge of his vision and the smell of some sharp antiseptic burned in his nose.

"Almost done," a voice said.

Noah shook his head violently. He staggered and fell to the ground, bruising his knees painfully on the blacktop. His surroundings had popped back into sharp focus, the grayness gone.

Noah climbed slowly to his feet and rubbed his aching knees. Another dream, he thought, disappointed. He couldn't fool himself anymore. Things were not getting better. These . . . *events* that happened while Noah was awake couldn't really be called *dreams*. He had seen other words in the books about abductees. *Attacks. Seizures.* Or maybe *psychotic episodes.* No matter which one you picked, they all meant that something was seriously wrong.

Still trembling, Noah started for home. He ran beside darkened windows and along empty sidewalks as he went past downtown Stone Harbor. As he passed an insurance company at the edge of town, he heard a car engine start up behind him. Noah glanced back and saw the dark shape of a long sedan emerge from a narrow alley between two buildings. It slid out onto the main road and turned in his direction. Its headlights were off. Instead of driving past him, the car approached in fits and starts, advancing ten or twenty feet, stopping, and then moving again.

At first Noah thought the car might be trying to find an address, or maybe it had a mechanical problem. He ran down the hill, passing old stone houses and rows of storm-twisted trees. At the foot of the hill, he turned left onto Cross Street. Ten seconds later, the car followed.

Noah swallowed hard. Half the people in town lived in the direction he was running. Just because the car was going this way didn't necessarily mean it was following him. He increased his pace, running hard enough to set his backpack bouncing against his shirt. Sweat began to trickle down his face.

Headlights flared behind him. The car began to draw closer. Its fitful movement grew more steady, and the distance between Noah and the car shrank rapidly.

Noah glanced around as he ran, squinting against the headlights, trying to get a better look at the car. Behind the painfully bright lights, the car was nothing but a vague dark form. Through the windshield, Noah thought he could just make out the silhouette of a driver.

He wanted to believe it was Josh, coming to offer another ride, or possibly his parents, out to see what was keeping him. But deep inside, Noah knew neither of these ideas was true.

The same part of his mind that had insisted for a week that someone was following him was now awake and screaming. There *was* someone following him. This was no dream.

Suddenly, a loud roar reverberated behind him. The car jumped forward, its engine racing. The headlights were centered right on Noah.

Caught in the glare of the lights, Noah felt the world start to slip away. Gray fog settled around him. The burning odor of antiseptic came over him. The ring of pale faces gathered near.

"No!" screamed Noah, shaking his head violently. "Not now!"

Abruptly, the fog lifted. The car was fifty feet away and closing fast. Twenty feet. Ten.

Noah flung himself toward the grass at the side of the road. As he fell, there was a jarring thump against his left heel that spun him around and dropped him hard to the ground. It took him several seconds to realize that the car had struck him a glancing blow. If he had hesitated even a fraction of a second longer, the collision would have been deadly.

Stunned, Noah rolled onto his back and sat up slowly.

The car charged on to the end of the block, then skidded to a halt. It sat there for a moment, the engine revving up to a whine, fading to a low rumble, then soaring up the scale again.

Noah got to his feet and walked slowly across the lawn. It seemed as if the night had grown an extra dimension. The air felt as thick as water. Everything along the street stood out with unreal clarity. He could feel the grass blades bending under his feet. He could smell someone cooking pot roast half a block away.

A light came on in a house down the road. The second that the light cut through the darkness, the car rumbled slowly away.

Noah ran after it. He reached the end of the block in time to see the square red flares of the car's brake lights as it slowed at the end of a long slope. Then the car turned off to the right and vanished. The rumble of its engine faded from the still night air.

In the sudden silence, Noah could hear his own heart pounding against his chest and his breath rasping in his lungs. He hadn't gotten a good look at the car. It was some dark color, he knew that much, and his impression was that it was an older sedan, maybe a four-door. More than that, he couldn't say.

"They tried to kill me," he whispered into the night. There was a sour, burning taste in his throat. His breath came out as puffs of white in the cooling air.

One part of his mind insisted that Noah couldn't know they were really trying to run him down. The car might have only been trying to frighten him, or the driver might not even have known Noah was there.

The other part of his brain, the part that he had been resisting for weeks, knew better. The car had followed him from town. It had probably been waiting for him to run past. They were trying to kill him. He had only two questions: Why? And who were *They?*

He was still jumpy when he reached his home and found Josh McQuinn's red Camaro waiting in the driveway. He stood for a moment, trying to determine if Josh's car might have been the one that tried to run him down. He didn't think it was. The car in the street had seemed larger, and there was no reason to suspect Josh other than the image from Noah's dream. But Noah no longer knew what part of the dreams it was safe to ignore.

Even before he pushed through the front door, Noah could hear laughter coming from the house. Inside, Noah found his parents sitting in the living room, with Josh McQuinn sprawled loosely in an armchair. Josh's long, thin arms dangled over the sides of the chair, and his narrow face was split by a grin. "That's what I told him," Josh was saying.

"Told who?" asked Noah. He stepped into the room and closed the door.

Noah's mother looked over at the sound of his entrance. "There you are," she said. She smiled brightly. "Look who's come to see you."

Noah nodded. "What's up, Josh?"

"Hi," said Josh. "I tried to catch you at school, but I couldn't find you."

"I saw your car," Noah told his friend. "We must have just missed each other."

"When I couldn't find you there, I thought I'd come by here and give you the good news," Josh said. He climbed out of the chair and stood grinning in the middle of the room. "I had another talk with Coach Harris this afternoon."

"And?"

"And he wants you back at practice on Monday," Josh finished with a big smile. "Congratulations, you're back on the team!"

Noah knew that he should have been excited, but he wasn't. Compared to the dreams and the car that had tried to kill him, playing on the basketball team suddenly didn't seem very important. He worked up a smile, hoping he didn't look as shaky as he felt.

"That's great," Noah said with as much enthusiasm as he could manage. "What did you say to get him to ease up?"

Josh climbed out of his chair and shrugged. "Nothing really. Like I said, Coach already knew that he needed you on the team."

"Don't be modest," Noah's father told Josh. "You've been a good friend to Noah. We all appreciate your help."

Josh looked down at the carpet and brushed a hand over his short pale hair. "Noah would have done the same thing for me."

Guilt stabbed at Noah's stomach. Only a few moments earlier, he had been wondering if Josh was trying to kill him, when all the time Josh had been thinking about how he could help Noah. Josh was a better friend than Noah deserved.

"Thanks," Noah told Josh softly. He affectionately punched his fist against the blue leather sleeve of Josh's letterman jacket. "I owe you."

"Naw," said Josh. "You come back and score a dozen points next week. That's all I want to see." He turned and nodded to Noah's parents. "I better get running. My mom will make me sleep in the garage if I don't get home soon."

"Well, you're always welcome here," said Noah's mother.

"I'll keep that in mind," Josh replied. "I might have to take you up on it one day." He leaned toward Noah and spoke softly. "Walk out with me. I've got some other news."

Noah nodded. "Back in a second," he called to his parents. Then he followed Josh out the front door.

Josh leaned against the side of his red car and crossed his arms. "Guess who else I talked to today?"

Noah shook his head. "I'm a rotten guesser."

"How about Dee's father?"

"Mr. Janes?" Noah frowned. In the summertime, Stone Harbor boasted a sizable police department to handle all the visitors, but Dee's father was the town's one and only year-round cop. "What did he want? Did he catch you tearing up the road in that car?"

Josh shook his head. "It wouldn't be the first time." He grinned for a moment, but his face quickly turned serious. "This time he didn't want to talk about me. He wanted to talk about *you*. You and Caroline."

Noah shook his head. "I don't understand."

"Caroline's missing." Josh leaned in close. "No one's seen her since last night."

A streak of cold shivered slowly down Noah's back. "What do you mean, *missing*?"

Josh snorted. "What do you think?" he answered. "I mean *gone*." He turned and looked around for a moment, as if making sure there was no one else around. "Mr. Janes says someone saw you and Caroline having a fight yesterday."

Noah squeezed his eyes shut and rubbed a hand across his face. It had to be the librarian. "We weren't really fighting," he explained.

"Yeah, well," said Josh, "whatever you were doing, that was the last time anyone remembers seeing Caroline."

The air turned thick in Noah's lungs. There was a sharp odor, and a murmur of distant voices.

Noah shook his head sharply, driving the dream away. "What did you tell him?"

Josh shrugged. "I told him that you and Caroline weren't dating anymore. I told him there was nothing between you."

"That's the truth," Noah said.

"Let's hope Mr. Janes believes it," said Josh. He pulled open the door of the Camaro. White light spilled out of the car. "He said that if Caroline doesn't show up tomorrow, he'll have to call the state cops."

Noah gritted his teeth. "Thanks for telling me."

Josh folded his long frame into the car seat. "I figured somebody better warn you before the FBI came swooping in." He tugged the door shut, gave a wave out the window, cranked the Camaro, and sped away.

Noah went back into the house and walked slowly up the stairs to his room. Thoughts of the mysterious, murderous car swirled in his mind, mixed with worry about Caroline. She might have just decided to skip out on school, or drive down to the nearest city, but Noah couldn't remember Caroline ever doing anything like that before. Somehow it seemed far too big a coincidence for this to be happening at the same time as everything else.

He sat down on the edge of the bed and leaned over with his hands on his knees. There had to be something he could do, some way to figure out what was happening.

A soft beeping from the computer alerted Noah that there was electronic mail waiting for him. He got up from the bed and walked over to his desk. With a click of the mouse, the message opened.

It was a very short message.

Stay away from Kathleen Davisidaro. You see her at the risk of your life. And hers.

SEVEN

For Harley, sleep was impossible.

The house on the Tulley Hill base had only been her home for two days. Without her father, it felt cold and alien. She wandered around the house all night, wishing the door would open and her father would walk in. Finally, she sat down in front of the television and watched the flickering screen for hours. The noise from the TV lent a little life to the empty house, but it did nothing to make Harley feel less lonely or frightened.

As gray dawn began to penetrate the woods, Harley went to the window and looked out across the lawn. Sometime during the night, the weather had turned cold. Frost glittered on the windshield of her father's car and on the chrome fenders of Harley's motorcycle. If she was going to go to school, Harley was going to have to break out some warmer clothes.

Most of Harley's things were still packed in cardboard boxes. She had to open half a dozen cartons before she found her sweaters and a light jacket. While she was getting dressed, she had a sudden, nagging thought. She walked down the hall to her father's room and looked inside.

Someone had been there.

The cardboard boxes that held her father's papers had been cut open. Their contents were spread over the bed and floor in careless heaps. Manila folders had been ripped open and tossed into the trash. Books lay spine-up with their pages crushed.

Harley stood in the doorway and stared. She didn't care what kind of emergency this trip had been, her father never would have left his papers this way. *Neatness* might as well have been his middle name.

She bent, picked up a pair of books from the floor, and carried them over to the bed. Whoever had gone through her father's room had not even tried to make it look like he had left on a trip. All the boxes marked Files or Books had been ripped open, but most of those marked as Clothing or Personal Belongings were still closed. Even the jacket her father had worn the day before was still hanging in the closet. In the bathroom, she found his toothbrush and shaving kit.

Harley went back out to her father's bedroom and sat down amid the heaps of paper. There was a tight, sick feeling in her throat as she tried to imagine what kind of assignment might have required her father to leave without even taking a change of clothes. She pressed her lips together in a hard line. There was no such assignment.

Colonel Braddock was lying.

For a moment, Harley wanted to throw herself down on the bed and cry, but a wave of anger burned through her fear. If she couldn't trust the commander to tell her what was really going on, then she would just have to find out on her own.

Harley looked around the room. Everything that she had left of her father was right here. If she was going to find any clues about what had happened, this was probably the best place to start looking.

She picked up all the fallen books and papers. Many of them were too technical for Harley to understand, but she sorted them as best she could. Next she cut open the boxes of clothing and personal things. She found souvenirs of the places where they had lived in the past in one box. In another were old pictures.

Harley paused to run her finger over yellowing pictures of herself as a child. Others showed Harley's mother. Her mother had been dead so long that Harley had only a vague recollection of a woman with sad, dark eyes. Her only other memories of her mother were actually memories of these photographs, which she had pored over as a child.

She put the pictures away and went across to the closet. Her father's checkbook was still in the pocket of his coat. So were his car keys. Her fingers touched something larger in the inside pocket of the coat. Harley reached in deep and pulled out a pair of small notebooks bound together with a rubber band.

Harley slid the rubber band free and opened the first book. Inside it looked like a diary. The first page had a date on it that was almost fifteen years ago. Below the date were words written in her father's small, neat handwriting.

Today was the breakthrough. Application seems to be the key. Results obtained represent strong potential for trans-alpha process . . .

Harley stopped reading. *Trans-alpha.* It was a strange phrase, but she was sure she had heard it before.

She frowned, trying to remember. Then it came to her.

"Noah," she whispered.

Noah had said something about trans-alpha while he was acting strange. But Harley couldn't begin to think of any way that what Noah had said could be connected to something her father had done fifteen years before.

Harley reached into the coat pocket one last time, and her hand closed on something cold and hard. She pulled it out and found herself looking at a black snub-nosed revolver.

She stared at the gun in shock. Harley had never known her father to carry a gun. He always said he hated guns. But there it was in her hand, as ugly and potent as a rattlesnake.

Harley laid the gun on the bed and closed her eyes. She had been looking for clues, but now that she had them, she didn't know what to do. After being up all night, she felt too exhausted to think.

From the far end of the house, she heard the buzz of the alarm clock in her own bedroom. School was only an hour or so away. Harley certainly didn't feel like going. Of course, if she didn't go, Colonel Braddock might say she wasn't following the rules. It might be all the excuse he needed to send Harley off to live with her aunt.

Which was exactly what Harley figured the commander wanted. If he could get Harley away from the base, there would be no one around to ask questions or get in the way.

She wasn't about to make it that easy for Braddock.

Harley got dressed and went to the bathroom to brush out her hair. The face in the mirror looked tired and worried. Just looking at herself made Harley feel like lying down for one, or two, or maybe ten hours.

She stuck her tongue out at the reflection in the glass. "Be tough," she told herself. The sound of her voice was strangely loud in the empty house.

There was no one in sight when Harley went outside to get on her bike. On the other side of the street were only the thick old elms and the tangled shadows that gathered on the forest floor. Nothing moved. Not even the tree limbs stirred in the cool air. But Harley felt as though a dozen eyes were focused on her.

She was about to leave when she thought of something. Harley got up from her bike and ran back inside. She picked up her father's journals from the bed and shoved them into her bag. After a moment's hesitation, she grabbed the revolver, too.

Still feeling as if she were being watched, Harley returned to her bike, pulled on her helmet, kicked the bike into life, and rolled out of the base. The feeling of being watched faded slowly as Harley drove down the road to Stone Harbor, but it didn't go away completely. She checked her mirror frequently to see if there really were someone behind her. The road was clear.

She reached school without seeing anything unusual, and was about to go into homeroom when Dee stopped her in the hall.

"Hey," Dee asked, her eyes burning with curiosity, and maybe a little jealousy. "How was your big date with Noah?"

"It wasn't a date," Harley replied. She turned around, looking at the students coming down the hallway. "We only went running together."

Between all the moving students, Harley spotted someone standing at the end of the hallway. A flash of dark blue clothing. It looked like one of the guards from the base. Maybe the one who had carried a clipboard. Harley stood on tiptoe, trying to see better.

A hand grabbed her by the arm and pulled her around. "Hello!" Dee blurted. "Hello? Earth to Harley. Did you hear anything I said?"

"What?" asked Harley. She looked over her shoulder, but the dark figure was gone.

"Wow," said Dee. "It's contagious."

Harley gave up looking for the figure in the hallway and turned her attention back to Dee. "What do you mean?"

"You and Noah. You hang out with him for one afternoon, and *wham*." Dee opened her eyes wide and stared across the hall. "Instant zombie."

"It's not Noah that's got me acting strange," said Harley. "It's my father."

"Your father?" Dee frowned. "Did he do something to you?"

"No, no. It's nothing like that," said Harley. She paused for a second. "My father is missing."

Dee's forehead creased with concern. "Missing?"

Harley nodded. "The people at the base say he's gone on some assignment. But it doesn't feel right." Harley quickly told Dee about her meeting with the base commander. The bell rang for the start of homeroom in the middle of the story, but neither Harley or Dee moved at the sound.

When Harley was done, all the other students had cleared out of the hallway. Dee looked thoughtful. "How are you going to find him?"

"I don't know," Harley admitted. "Before this, the military was always just someplace where my dad worked. I've never had to think about how to get information out of them."

Dee leaned back against the lockers. "It just so happens that I might be able to help."

"How?"

"I know someone that knows ways to handle these things." Dee mimicked tipping a hat down over her eyes and brought her hand to her mouth to remove an invisible cigarette. Her voice took on the gravelly tone of some detective from an old black-and-white movie. "I can make a few inquiries. Follow some leads. Look under a few rocks."

Despite her worries, Harley had to smile. "How are you going to do all that?"

"Easy," Dee replied. She straightened and pushed herself away from the lockers. "My dad is Stone Harbor's police chief."

Harley felt a surge of hope. "You really think he can help?" she asked.

"I don't know for sure," Dee admitted. "Finding people is part of his job, but those military guys might get in the way." She shrugged. "Won't hurt to find out. We'll go see my dad after school."

Throughout the school day Harley tried to think of what she was going to tell Dee's father. It was hard to find a balance between showing how worried she was and sounding like she was imagining some big conspiracy.

When Noah sat down in front of her in English class, Harley had to bite her lip to keep from asking him what *trans-alpha* meant. She expected Noah to ask about the car that had come to collect her. He asked nothing. He sat down at his desk without even turning to look at Harley.

When the bell rang, Noah was up and out of his seat like a shot. Harley called out his name, but Noah didn't even turn. He pushed his way through the other students and plunged into the hall.

Harley scowled after him. She picked up her own books and was about to leave when she noticed a small piece of paper folded in the seat of Noah's desk. On it was the single letter *H*.

She looked around to make sure that no other students were watching, then bent down to grab the piece of paper. Without stopping, she shoved it into her books and walked out of the room. Only when she was down the hall and out of sight did she unfold the little square. Inside was a single line of writing.

I need to see you. Meet on pier. 6 P.M.

Harley wadded up the slip of paper and shoved it into the nearest trash bin. For a moment, she felt like laughing. It was all getting too strange too fast. She felt like she was lost in the middle of some old spy novel.

Dee was waiting for Harley at her locker. "Do you have track team practice today?"

Harley thought about it for a moment, then shook her head. "I don't think so. Anyway, I forgot to bring my stuff."

"Good," said Dee. "We'll go straight to see my dad. Maybe he can crack this case before supper."

Dee rode behind Harley to the city building in the middle of Stone Harbor. It was a simple but solid-looking building with a front that appeared to have been carved from one massive sheet of granite. In the rear corner of the building was a small office with a door of pebbly glass and the word Police written in plain black letters. Behind the front desk sat a man with sandy brown hair and a round, open face. He wore a blue police uniform with a silver shield-shaped badge on his chest.

The man looked up as they came through the door. "Uh-oh," he said. "This obviously means trouble."

"You bet," said Dee. "Dad, this is my friend Harley. Harley, this is my dad."

The policeman stood up and came over to shake Harley's hand. "Charles Janes," he introduced himself. "Good to meet you. Dee's been talking about you all week."

"She has?"

Dee's father laughed. "Don't worry. Dee's always going on about something."

Dee cleared her throat loudly. "Harley has a problem," she said.

"Oh?" Mr. Janes looked at Harley. "What's wrong?"

Harley took a deep breath. "It's my father," she

81

said. "He's a contract worker for the military. We moved here last week so he could take a job at Tulley Hill Research Facility."

At the name of the base, Dee's father frowned. "I know the place," he said. "Go on."

"My father is . . ." Harley stopped and looked down at the floor for a moment. She had to be careful. "I mean, my father didn't come home last night. The base commander told me that my dad had been sent off on some assignment."

"Braddock told you this?" asked Dee's father.

"Yeah."

"And did he say where your father had been assigned?"

"No," Harley replied. "And they wouldn't say for how long."

Mr. Janes rubbed his chin. "All right, go on."

Harley took a breath and continued. "Well, whatever happened to my dad, he didn't even get a chance to tell me he was leaving. His car's still in the driveway. All his clothes are still in the house."

Mr. Janes waited until Harley had been silent for a few seconds. "Is that it?" he asked at last.

Harley thought of the two books she had stuffed into her bag. And of the revolver. Both of them would surely interest the policeman. But Harley wasn't ready to give up—or mention—either the books or the gun until she knew something about what they meant.

"That's it," she said.

Dee's father nodded and walked over to his desk. He picked up a foam cup of coffee and took a long drink. "All right," he said at last. "I'll tell you right off there's not a lot I can do. If your dad had disappeared anywhere else, I could declare him a missing person. Even then, I'd have to wait forty-eight hours before I could file a report. But since he vanished on a military base, he's not really missing."

"He *is* missing," Harley insisted.

"Nope," Mr. Janes said. "Until the base says he's missing, he's not missing."

Harley's heart sank. "But they're not going to declare him missing," she said. "They're covering up something."

"It wouldn't be the first time," said Mr. Janes. He put the coffee down on the counter and looked into Harley's eyes. Despite his round, almost boyish face, Harley could see a hardness in Dee's father. He might be one man in a small room, but he was the police in Stone Harbor, and he knew his job. "That base out there is in the business of hiding secrets," he said. "They don't like sharing with anyone, not even the police."

"So there's nothing you can do?" Harley asked.

The policeman shook his head. "Officially, it's probably best I don't start any paperwork on this. Unofficially, I can make some inquiries. Who knows? We might get lucky."

A tightness pulled around Harley's chest and she was suddenly afraid she was going to cry. "Thank you," she whispered.

"Hey, you're a friend of Dee's." Mr. Janes drained the last of his coffee and crushed the empty cup in his hand. "Besides, I've got my own problems with good old Colonel Braddock. I don't even want to *think* of the zoning infractions he's committed with his renovation of the base."

A new thought came to Harley. "Will the commander know you're looking into this? He's already started talking about making me leave the base. I'm afraid if he knows I talked to you, he'll have my bags packed tonight."

"Don't worry about that," Dee's father replied. "The military aren't the only ones who know how to keep a secret." He looked around at Dee. "Why don't you invite Harley over for dinner?"

"Cool," said Dee. "Come. Eat. Watch the tube with the rest of the tribe."

"Um, I can't," said Harley. "Not tonight."

"Another date with Noah?"

Harley shook her head. "Definitely not a date," she said.

"Another mystery," Dee sighed. "Well, come on and drive me home. I can tempt you with thoughts of hot meals along the way."

Harley said good-bye to Dee's father and drove Dee across town to her house. The thought of going in and having a real meal *was* tempting. Harley's father usually did the cooking around their house. She tried to remember if she had eaten either breakfast or dinner the night before. From the way her stomach was growling, the answer was probably no.

After dropping Dee off, Harley turned the motorcycle around and went back through downtown Stone Harbor and out to the pier. The beachfront was almost as deserted as it had been the day before.

Dull red sunlight slipped through the skeleton of

the closed roller coaster, crisscrossing the sand with twisting black shadows. A crisp wind off the sea whistled over the pier and raised whitecaps on the water. Down on the beach, a man with a metal detector walked slowly along the waterline. From what Harley could see, he didn't seem to be having much luck.

The sun dropped down behind the hills to the west, leaving the waterfront in purple gloom. Miles up the coast, the beam of an old lighthouse slipped out across the water.

Harley left her bike near the foot of the pier and walked out to where the water surged under her feet. She closed her eyes and leaned against a piling. It seemed like only a moment later that she was awakened by the sound of someone thumping along the boards. She opened her eyes to find that it was completely dark.

A shadowy figure stood ten feet away.

Harley stepped back. Her hand went to her bag, feeling for the compact bulk of the gun inside. "Who's there?" she demanded.

"It's me," replied a whispered voice.

The figure stepped closer. In the faint light of the rising moon, she saw Noah's strong, handsome face. "Come on," said Noah. "I've got my car down by the road. We've got to get out of here."

Harley squinted at him in the darkness. "I thought we were going to talk here."

"We were," said Noah. "But I'm not sure that it's safe to stay. Come on, we need to get out of here before they find me."

There was an edge in his voice that made Harley

take another step back. "Before who finds you?" she asked.

"I'll tell you in the car," said Noah. He came toward Harley again. The boards of the pier creaked softly under his feet. "Look. I'm in danger. And I think you are, too."

"What kind of danger?" asked Harley.

"The kind where someone wants to kill you," replied Noah.

"No," said Harley. "No one wants to kill me."

Noah ran his hands over his face. He stared down at the boards for a moment before talking. "You may be right," he said. "Maybe I'm just crazy." He looked up, his blue eyes almost black in the dim light. "But maybe I'm not crazy. Do you want to take that chance? We're talking about your *life*."

Harley followed him back to the car.

EIGHT

Noah turned off the main road onto a country route that was nothing more than a scattering of gravel over a pair of deep ruts.

Harley gripped the edge of the dashboard and held on as the car bounced along the rough track. "Where are we going?"

"Nowhere," said Noah. "I'm just trying to get far enough away from the highway to be out of sight." He drove on until they reached a wide place where an old leaning shack was slowly crumbling into dust. Noah pulled the car over to the side of the road, turned off the lights, and killed the engine.

Harley looked at him with fire in her dark eyes. "This better not be some stupid scheme for getting me into the backseat. If it is, you may as well turn around now."

"It's not," Noah said.

"It better not be." Harley pushed her long black hair away from her face. "Why did you want to talk to me?"

Noah frowned. "Maybe I shouldn't tell you about this, but I thought I owed it to you." He reached down beside his seat and pulled out a sheet of paper. He flipped on the light inside the car and handed the paper to Harley. "Read this."

Harley took the paper and glanced at it. "Where did you get this?"

"It's a hard copy of my E-mail," said Noah. "Whoever sent it worked hard to keep me from finding out where it came from."

"You see her at the risk of her life," quoted Harley. She looked up from the paper. "How do I know this is real?" she asked. "You could have made it up yourself."

Noah shook his head. "I didn't write it. I can't prove it, but that's the truth."

Harley looked at him for a moment, then handed the paper back. "Let's say I believe you. You think this is serious?"

"Pretty serious." Noah took the paper and shoved it into his pocket. "Someone tried to run me down last night on the way home."

"What?" Harley stared at him with her mouth hanging open. "Every time I think that things have gotten about as crazy as possible, they get even crazier. Who could possibly care that we went running together?"

"I don't know," said Noah. "I mean, I've got some ex-girlfriends, but none of them are quite whacked enough to do something like this."

Harley laughed, but it was a laugh edged with more exhaustion than humor. "So who then?"

Noah took a deep breath. "I think it has to do with my dreams."

"Dreams?" said Harley. "How can dreams have anything to do with someone wanting to kill you?"

There was a glow of headlights behind them as a car passed on the main highway. Noah watched in the rearview mirror until he was sure the car had gone past their hiding place. "I'm not sure how long we have," he said. "I'm going to tell you this as flat as I can. When I'm done, you can tell me I'm nuts. I don't care."

"All right," said Harley. She shifted in the car seat. "Go ahead."

Noah nodded. "The dreams began about three weeks ago." He went on to describe the glowing faces with their huge dark eyes, the human doctor, the flashing knife, and the terrible fear that accompanied the mysterious and horrifying images. He didn't mention Josh. Noah had no idea what seeing Josh in the dreams meant. There was no reason for him to think Josh was really involved at all.

"The dreams are all the same," he said. "Sometimes I remember more of them, sometimes less. At first they only came at night. But the last few days, the images keep coming at me even when I'm awake."

"Is that what you were doing yesterday?" asked Harley. "Is that what was bothering you when we were running through town?"

Noah nodded. "I had a flash then. I remembered something new."

Harley looked down at the floorboard, the dark wings of her hair sliding forward to veil her face. "Okay," she said. "You've been having weird dreams about little guys with big heads. They're still just dreams. How can this have anything to do with someone trying to run you over?"

"Because I don't think they're just dreams," Noah replied.

"What else could they be?"

"Memories."

"Memories of what?" Harley asked.

Noah ran a hand through his floppy hair. "Of an abduction."

"You were kidnapped?"

"Yes," said Noah. "In a way. But not by people."

Harley tilted her head to the side and looked at Noah with an expression he couldn't decipher. "Aliens," she said.

Now that someone else had said it, Noah found the word ridiculous. He wanted to say *no*. He never believed he had been kidnapped by creatures from another planet. How could he? The whole idea was too silly to even think about.

"Yes," he said softly. "That's what I think."

There was a minute of painful silence before Harley spoke again. "I've heard of things like this," she said. "Aliens. UFO's. I've seen them all over the tabloid papers, and on television. But I've never met anyone that said it happened to them. I've never even met anyone that thought it was real."

"Now you have," said Noah.

"Do you have any evidence?"

"No. That is, unless you consider the message and someone trying to kill me as evidence."

Harley gave another ragged laugh. "It's evidence of something, I guess." She turned and looked straight into Noah's eyes. "Say I did believe you. Say I believed every word of it. What then?"

"Then I'd . . ." Noah stopped. For the first time, he realized he had been expecting to fail. He had planned a hundred things to say to Harley when she didn't believe him. He hadn't thought of anything to say to her if she did. "I don't know what comes next," he admitted. "I never thought you might believe me."

"I didn't say I did believe you," Harley reminded him. She looked away from Noah, her face a silhouette against the darkness. "Tell me," she said. "What does *trans-alpha* mean?"

Noah frowned. "What?"

Harley turned around in the seat and looked straight into his face. Her eyes were as black as the night outside. "Trans-alpha."

"Never heard of it," said Noah.

"I think you have," Harley contradicted him. "You said something about it yesterday while you were remembering your dream."

Noah rubbed his chin. He tried to remember the voices in his dream, but the words all ran together. "Are you sure?"

"Yes," Harley replied. "*Trans-alpha patterns*, that's what you said. Do you know what it means?"

The words did sound strangely familiar, but Noah had no idea how or why. "No," he answered. "No, I don't."

Harley slumped in her seat. "You have to know something," she said. "It's all I've got."

"Why is this trans-alpha so important?" asked Noah. "Do *you* know what it means?"

"No, but . . ." Harley suddenly pounded her fists against the dashboard of the car. "You have to know something!"

Noah leaned away, staring at her in surprise. "I

don't know," he said. "I'm sorry, but I just don't."

"My father is missing," Harley told him flatly. She stared off into the darkness. "That's why those guys from the base came and picked me up last night. They say he's gone on some assignment." Harley gave a sour laugh. Then she lowered her face in her hands.

After a silent moment, Noah reached out and touched Harley on the arm. "I'm sorry," he said. "You think he's okay?"

"I don't know," Harley admitted. "I don't know where he is. I don't know *how* he is. I don't even know if he's still . . ." She stopped and shook her head violently. "I don't know anything!"

"What about the trans-alpha business?" Noah asked. "You think that has something to do with your dad?"

Harley nodded. "It's in some of his papers."

Noah thought about it for a moment. "What did your father do at the base?"

"He's an electronics expert," Harley answered. "RADAR systems. Computers. That kind of thing."

"Maybe he's working on something to do with alien technology," suggested Noah.

Harley shook her head so hard that her hair fanned out around her face. "I'm sorry, but that's too much. I don't believe in little aliens with big heads, I don't believe you've been abducted by some mysterious force, and I don't believe my father has been working on UFO's."

"What about the note? What about the car that tried to run me over?"

"Don't take this the wrong way," Harley said.

"But I didn't see the car. And you said yourself you couldn't prove the note was real."

"You really don't believe me." Noah's eyes squinted in disappointment.

"How can I?" Harley reached over and took Noah's hand. "Before you had these dreams, would you have believed it if someone told you the same story?"

Noah wanted to argue. He wanted to *make* her believe him. Instead he shook his head and sighed. "No," he said. "No, I guess I wouldn't. So what do we do now?"

Harley withdrew her hand. "Please take me back to my bike," she said. "If you don't know what trans-alpha means, I need to find out someone who . . . someone who . . ." She stopped and leaned forward. "What's that sound?"

At first Noah could barely hear the noise, but it quickly grew louder. It started as a hum, but in a moment it was a pulsing, pounding throb that shook the car.

A dazzling light suddenly lit up the field ahead of them. A brilliant circle of white slid over the old shack, moved toward them over the ground, then moved off into the field. A few seconds later, it turned and began to move slowly back toward the car. In the sky above, Noah saw a vague dark shape moving against the stars.

"What is it?" Harley asked. "A search helicopter?"

"I don't know," Noah said. "But I think this is a pretty good sign that we should leave."

He cranked up the car, threw it into reverse, and

turned around. The circle of light brushed over the rotten building and swept on into a grove of small trees at the side of the road. Noah slammed the transmission straight from neutral into second and pushed the gas pedal to the floor. He kept the headlights off. The wheels bumped, jittered, and caught on the dirt and gravel road. The steering wheel jumped in his hands as Noah struggled to keep the Mustang on the bumpy track.

Harley twisted around in her seat. "If they saw us, they don't seem to be following us."

They reached the main road. Noah stopped for a moment and watched the light moving back and forth over the field. Whatever was shining that brilliant beam onto the ground, Noah couldn't make it out. "That didn't look like any helicopter I ever saw," he said.

"Well, whatever it is," said Harley. "It's coming this way."

Noah glanced back and saw that the circle of light was moving quickly in their direction. He flipped on the headlights and roared off down the main road, shifting through the gears as he brought the Mustang up to speed.

Harley kept watch out the back. "It's getting closer," she warned.

Noah ground the gas pedal into the carpet, urging the car past eighty miles an hour, then ninety.

"Still closing!" shouted Harley. "It's going to catch us."

Noah glanced in the side mirror and saw the gleam of the spotlight only a car length behind. "Hang on!"

He punched off the headlights. The sudden darkness seemed as black as the inside of a barrel. Noah stomped the brakes, then jerked the wheel hard to the right.

The tires screamed in protest as the Mustang spun around. For a fraction of a second, the spotlight swept over the car. The brightness was like nothing Noah had ever experienced before. The light wasn't just around him, it was *in* him. It seemed to shine right through the roof of the car. Right through his eyelids. Right through his *bones*.

Noah stomped the gas again and they went racing back in the other direction.

"What was that?" Harley asked. Her voice was a harsh whisper.

"Is it still behind us?"

Harley turned around to look. "Yes," she replied. "It's going the other way. No, wait . . . Now it's coming toward us again."

Noah threw the car into a turn. In the darkness he could barely see the gleam of the steel railing that separated the roadway from the sea. "We only need a few minutes," he said. "I've got an idea."

Harley tugged on her seat belt. "I hope you know this road really, really well."

The light began to draw close again. It was only twenty feet behind them when Noah crushed the brakes and turned the car down another narrow dirt road. They jarred along, hitting bumps so hard that they drove Noah's head into the roof.

"Where is it now?" he asked.

"The light's stopped by the side of the road," said

Harley. "It's going back and forth, like it's looking for us."

"Ten more seconds and we'll be under cover," Noah told her. He skirted around a huge pothole and caught sight of what he had been looking for. Up ahead, the main highway cut over the ragged track they were following, rising above it in a concrete overpass. Noah shot under the bridge and pulled as far over to the side as he could. Then he killed the engine.

"Can you still see it?" he asked.

Harley shook her head. "I think it's gone."

Noah leaned back in his chair and let out a ragged breath. "If you don't mind, I think we should stay here for a while, just to be sure."

For a minute or more, neither of them spoke. Finally, Harley broke the silence. "It had to be a helicopter," she said softly.

"Maybe it was," said Noah. "Whatever it was, it was definitely after us."

"You weren't kidding, were you?" Harley asked. "The note. The car that tried to kill you. Your feeling that you're being followed. That stuff was real."

"Yes," Noah replied, turning to look at her face in the darkness. "And your father's not the only one that's missing. One of the girls from school, a girl I used to date, has been missing for two days."

"You think that has something to do with all the rest of this?"

Noah shrugged. "I'm not sure," he said, "but, yeah. I think it does."

Harley bit her lip. "Dee was right."

"What?"

"Dee said your craziness was contagious," said Harley. "She was right." Harley put her hand against her forehead. "But I still don't believe in aliens. Whatever is going on, that can't be it."

"Fine," Noah told her. "It doesn't matter to me whether you really believe that part or not. All that matters is that you know there's someone out there who's worried about us being together."

"It still doesn't make any sense," said Harley. "Maybe something important is in your dreams, but I don't have any dreams. I'm only a high-school student. About the only unusual thing I know is how to fix old motorcycles. I'm not dangerous to anyone."

"Maybe they don't know that," said Noah. "Maybe they think your father talked to you about what he was working on."

Harley turned to look at Noah. "The base," she said.

"What?"

"My father may not be on assignment," Harley said, "but Colonel Braddock knows where he is. If all this has something to do with my father's work, then it has to have something to do with Tulley Hill Base."

Noah thought for a second. "Do you have a car?"

"Yes," replied Harley. "My father's car."

"Good." Noah tapped a finger against the steering wheel as he tried to make up a plan in the space of a few seconds. "Drive it to the grocery store tomorrow," he said at last. "The little store downtown. You know the one I mean?"

"Yes," Harley said. "Then what?"

"I'll meet you there." Noah started the car and

pulled out from their hiding place beneath the overpass. There was no sign of the strange light. "Then we'll go have a good look at the base."

Harley nodded. "All right." She reached into her handbag and produced something that glittered in the dark. It took Noah several seconds to realize that it was a pistol.

He jerked the Mustang to a stop. "What are you doing with that?"

"I found it with my father's things," said Harley. She turned the gun over in her hands. "It frightened me at first," she said, "but now I'm glad we've got it."

"You better be careful with that," Noah warned.

Harley shoved the gun back into her bag. "Tell that to the people who took my father," she said. "They're the ones who need to be careful."

Harley wondered if she was coming down with the flu. Her head was pounding. Her arms and legs ached as if she had been beaten from head to foot.

She sat in the living room of the house, staring out the window at the darkness. Earlier Harley had been exhausted, but now she felt wide awake. So awake that it was hard to imagine she would ever sleep again.

Everything kept turning over and over in her mind. Her father. Noah. The light. Trans-alpha pattern. The death threat.

It still didn't make sense. None of it made sense. In two days, Harley's life had drifted from normal to insane. She wished she could go back to Edwards. She wished she could get on her motorcycle and drive far away from Stone Harbor.

She wished her father was home.

Finally, when the night had worn on so long that it had almost become day again, Harley leaned against the side of the couch and drifted into a sleep full of nightmares.

The ringing of the phone woke her up. A quick glance at the clock in the kitchen showed that it was almost noon. She had slept for nine hours. Harley let the phone ring again while she stretched. Then she grabbed it off the hook.

"Hello?"

For a second, there was nothing on the other end of the phone but a faint warbling whine. Finally, a voice spoke. "Good morning, Ms. Davisidaro." It was a strange voice, full of buzzing and vibration. Harley couldn't even have said if it was male or female. It sounded like a voice being played off an old cheap radio.

"Who is this?" asked Harley.

"Someone who wants to help you," the voice replied. "And you *do* need help, Harley."

"Noa . . ." She caught herself before she finished blurting out Noah's name. "No," she said instead. "No, I don't think I need any help."

There was laughter over the phone—laughter as metallic and inhuman as an aluminum can being crushed. "Oh, I guess you don't care what happens to your *father* then, is that right?" the voice said.

Harley gripped the phone so tight she was surprised the plastic didn't crack. "What do you know about my father?"

"I know he's missing. I know Unit 17 isn't telling you anything."

"Do you know where he is?" asked Harley.

"No," the voice replied. "But I think we can find out."

"When?"

"Soon," said the voice. "Very soon. As soon as you take care of a little business for me."

There was a lump in Harley's throat. She swallowed and tried to stay calm. "What do you want me to do?" she asked.

There was a click and the humming sound died. A moment later, a dial tone came from the phone, just as if there had never been an incoming call.

100

Harley set the phone down in its cradle and stared at it. Whoever had made the call, he or she knew about her father's disappearance. For several minutes she sat beside the phone, hoping for another call, but none came.

A glance at the clock showed it was getting close to the time she was supposed to meet Noah. Harley checked the locks on the doors to make sure they were all secure, and then she took a quick shower. By the time she got her clothes on and dried her hair, she felt a little better. She went back into the living room and looked at her father's car sitting in the driveway.

A green sedan with a small gold triangle on the side went past on the road going into the base. A moment later a second followed. And a third. Harley leaned against the cold window glass watching them move away between the trees. The houses and the commander's office were all she had seen of Tulley Hill, but there had to be more. Somewhere in the base was the thing they had her father working on. The thing he couldn't talk about. Whatever was going on, it had started here.

She grabbed her leather jacket and retrieved her father's car keys from his bedroom. In a moment, she was out the door and on her way into Stone Harbor.

The Square Deal Grocery was no supermarket. The whole place had only two aisles, and the selection was limited to the basics. Harley filled four bags with bread, milk, cereal, and all the other staples it took to stock a kitchen. She took her time, glancing behind her to see if Noah was around. There was no sign of him.

After paying, Harley took the groceries outside and popped the trunk of her father's white car. She was about to put the last bag into the trunk when she heard a hiss from low on her right.

Noah was there, crouching beside her car. He wore a black sweatsuit, and he carried a dark brown leather backpack in one hand. "I'm glad to see you," he whispered. "I was beginning to think you weren't coming."

Harley glanced around. A few cars drove slowly past. Noah was out of sight from the street, but a half-dozen shoppers were still browsing inside the grocery store. At any moment one of them might look up and see him.

"Get in the car," Harley whispered back. "We'll talk once we get out of here."

Noah reached up and opened the passenger door. He eased inside and shut it softly, slumping down until only the very top of his head could be seen through the window. Harley put away the last of the groceries, slammed the trunk, and joined him. She turned the car south, back toward the base.

"Do you have a place we can go once we're inside the base?" Noah asked. "Somewhere I can hide?"

"They assigned us a house," Harley answered. "There are some other houses beside it, but I don't think anyone's in them. At least I haven't *seen* anyone."

"Good," said Noah. "We can wait there for it to get dark."

"What do we do once it's dark?"

"We see what we can find out about the base." Noah raised up for a moment and peeked out the window. "Pull over here," he said.

Harley looked around. There wasn't a house or any other building in sight. "Why here?"

"I need to get in the trunk," Noah answered. "If it is someone on the base who doesn't want us together, I can't really sign in at the front gate as your guest."

"Right you are," Harley replied.

Gravel crunched under the wheels of the car as Harley pulled over onto the shoulder. She opened the trunk and stood at the edge of the highway. Noah pushed some of the groceries out of the way and shoved himself as far back into the trunk as he could. His long legs ended up wrapped around the spare tire. When he was completely in, Harley rearranged the groceries to cover him.

"How does it look?" asked Noah. "Can you see me?"

Harley frowned. "Not if I don't look closely."

"If you do look closely?"

"Then we're both going to see what the inside of a military prison looks like," Harley told him. She shut the trunk, got back in the car, and drove on.

Another of the green sedans was waiting at the gate when Harley drove up. She pulled her father's car in behind it and waited. Sweat rose on Harley's forehead as she watched the guard looking through the trunk of the car ahead. The guard slammed the trunk and went back to the blockhouse. With a whir of electric motors, the gate rolled open and the sedan drove through.

Harley thought about turning around. It might look suspicious, but if anyone asked she could say she had forgotten something. She had her hand on the gearshift, ready to back up, when she realized it was too late. The guard was already walking toward her car.

The guard was one of the two that she had met when she'd first arrived at the base. It was the taller one, the one who looked like he lifted weights. He tapped his finger against the glass and waited while Harley rolled down the window.

"Morning," he said. "You want to pull on forward?"

Harley nodded. She felt like she was going to be sick, but she eased the car up to the gate.

The guard followed. "You have your pass card?" He took the piece of red plastic from Harley, looked at it quickly, and handed it back. "I'm afraid I'm going to have to ask you to get out of the car," he said. "We've got orders to search everyone this morning."

Wondering what the guard's reaction would be if she fainted in front of him, Harley opened her door and got out. The guard stepped past her and looked around the car. "All by yourself today?" he asked.

"Yes," Harley answered. Even to her own ears, her voice sounded like a frightened squeak.

The guard went around to the back of the car. "Can you open this trunk?"

"Sure," said Harley. She pulled out the keys and took them around to the back. The sooner this is over with, she thought, the sooner Noah and I can be lined up in front of a firing squad.

The trunk swung open, revealing the line of grocery bags.

The guard glanced down. "Looks like you've been doing some shopping," he said. "Where's your father? I'm surprised he's not with you."

"He's . . . he's on assignment," said Harley. "He may be away for a few days."

"Oh, yeah?" The guard straightened up, then leaned toward Harley. His square-jawed face brightened with a smile. "You mean to say you're all alone in there?"

Harley realized the guard had interests other than searching her car. She looked up into the guard's green eyes and smiled. "You know, your uniforms don't have name tags. I don't even know your name."

"Well," the guard said slowly. "We're not really supposed to tell our names." He looked around, then gave Harley a sly grin. "Wilkinson," said the guard. "Rudy Wilkinson."

"Rudy," said Harley, giving the name a little extra roll around her mouth. "You know, Rudy, it does get pretty lonely in here."

The guard looked around again, then turned back to Harley. "Maybe I could come by your house," he said. "I could, you know, help out with things while your father's away."

Harley put her hand against the guard's chest. It was like touching a brick wall. "I'm going to be a little busy tonight. I've still got some things to put away. But maybe later this week?" She blinked her eyes and smiled up at the guard.

Rudy Wilkinson might have been roughly the size of a tank, but that didn't stop him from blushing. "Sure," he said. "You mind if I call you?"

"No," said Harley. "I'd like that."

The guard's smile spread from ear to ear. "Well then, I'll be calling you." Another car pulled in behind Harley. The guard glanced back toward it. "I guess I better pass you on through," he said.

Harley reached up and closed the trunk. "I guess you better," she said, trying to sound disappointed.

"I'll see you soon."

"You bet," said the guard. He gave Harley a final smile and trotted over to the guard post.

Harley climbed into the car and cranked up the engine. As soon as the gate rolled back, she squeezed through and drove on to her house. By the time she got halfway there, she was laughing with relief. She laughed so hard that tears rolled down her face.

When they reached the house, Harley checked to make sure the coast was clear, then released Noah from the trunk.

He frowned at Harley. "Sounds like you were having fun back there."

"Oh, sure," said Harley. "I only wish I could share the fun with you." She looked down the road toward the gate. "I'm going to be avoiding that guy for the rest of the time I live here. This trip better be worth it." Together they picked up the groceries and hurried to the door.

Noah looked around as he carried the groceries to the kitchen. "I didn't know houses on military bases were this nice."

"They're not," said Harley. "At least, not usually." She put away the last of the groceries and closed the cabinet. "Now that you're in here, what's your great plan?"

Noah put his backpack down on the table and opened the zippered pocket. From the interior, he took out a sheet of paper and unfolded it on the table. "Take a look at this."

Harley squinted at the paper. It was covered in the thin squiggles of contour lines and patches of green. "Is this a map of the base?"

"Absolutely," said Noah. He tapped his finger

against the paper. "This little square here is the house we're in. This big grouping of buildings further in is where I think we should look first."

Harley picked up the corner of the map. "Where did you get this stuff? I thought this was a top-secret base."

"I got it over the Internet," said Noah. "I checked last night, and it turns out that Tulley Hill has been mentioned several times as a possible alien research facility. One of the FTP sites had these plans that date back to when this was an energy department complex."

"If this is such a big alien site," Harley asked, "then why didn't you know about it before?"

Noah shrugged. "I didn't look. I was only checking out abductions, not the rest of it."

For a moment Harley wondered again if Noah was faking all this. She watched him as he drew lines along the map. She hadn't checked on any of the things Noah had said. Maybe there was no missing girl. Maybe there weren't even any dreams. Maybe Noah was just as crazy as people said.

He looked up from the map and turned to face Harley. "What? Is something wrong?"

Harley shook her head and worked up a smile. "No," she said. "Just thinking."

Noah nodded and turned back to the map.

"Now we wait for it to get dark," Noah instructed. "Then we'll find out what's really going on around here."

"Fine," Harley agreed. She was relieved to hear how calm her voice sounded. But inside she was more afraid than she had ever been in her life.

TEN

Noah sat at the front window and stared between the slats of the venetian blinds. "We'd better wait at least a couple of hours until it's good and dark."

Harley came out of her bedroom wearing dark jeans and a black sweater. "You think this will do?" she asked.

"Oh, yeah," Noah said. "I think it'll do fine." The dark outfit might have been designed to keep her hidden, but that didn't stop Noah from admiring the way it fit Harley's trim figure.

Noah went over to the television and started going through the channels. He stopped at an old black-and-white movie. "Great," he said sarcastically. "A Hitchcock film. Just what we need to calm down."

"Leave it there," Harley ordered. She sat down on the couch. "This is one of my favorites."

Noah shrugged and joined her on the couch. He sat close enough to Harley to feel her warmth.

Waiting for it to be time for them to search the base, Noah would have sworn he'd be too nervous to watch anything on television, but he soon found himself caught up in the movie. In the film, Cary Grant played a regular guy who had fallen in with a nest of spies and counterspies. On another day, it might have seemed unbelievable. Now it seemed all too normal.

Halfway through the film, Harley leaned against Noah's shoulder. Noah was surprised, but he slipped his arm around her. She did nothing to stop him. By the time the hero of the movie was being chased by a crop duster plane, Harley's head was resting against Noah's chest.

Noah ran his hand along the smooth sleeve of Harley's sweater. She mumbled something softly and touched his fingers gently with hers. Noah was just about to lean down and kiss her, when he realized Harley was sound asleep. Noah pressed his lips lightly to the warm, dark hair at the crown of Harley's head. Then he leaned back against the soft cushions of the couch. In a moment, he was asleep himself.

When the dreams jerked Noah out of his slumber, Harley was gone. The television was droning on, full of people cheering for some stupid exercise contraption on an infomercial.

Noah got up, stretched, and rubbed the sleep out of his eyes. "Harley?"

"In here," she said.

He found Harley sitting beside the front window, staring out into the darkness. "What time is it?" Noah asked.

"Just after midnight," Harley replied. "We slept for over four hours."

"I'm sorry," said Noah. "I didn't mean to fall asleep."

Harley laughed. "And I did?" She shook her head. "My guts must trust you more than my head does. I don't think I've ever gone to sleep right beside someone before, except for my father."

"It must be my stimulating personality." Noah grinned. "Anyway, you won't mind if I go back to school and tell the guys we slept together, right?"

"No, I don't mind," Harley said calmly. "That is, not so long as you don't mind me trying out my pistol on your thick skull."

"Uh . . . maybe I'll stay quiet."

Harley nodded. "I think that might be best."

The short exchange with Harley made Noah feel better. It was the first time they had joked with each other. The short nap seemed to have done both of them good.

"Are you ready to go out there?" asked Noah.

"No," Harley answered. "But I guess I'll go anyway."

"We need to turn the lights out," Noah told her. "So our eyes can get adjusted before we go outside."

Harley walked around the house, flipping switches. Noah folded the map and put it in the pocket of his sweatsuit jacket. Then he turned off the television and the lights in the living room. When the house was completely dark, he returned to the window. Out beyond the trees was a vague glow of blue-white light.

Harley came up beside him so quietly that Noah jumped when she spoke. "Ready?"

"As I'll ever be," said Noah, turning to face her. He blinked, trying to see more clearly in the dark. "Are you bringing the gun?"

"No," Harley replied. "I don't think I'm ready to shoot anyone, and carrying a gun that you're not going to use sounds like a bad idea."

"You're probably right about that." Noah eased the front door open and slipped out into the night.

There was no sound but the faint breeze whispering between the trees and the occasional call of a distant owl. A thin fingernail of yellow moon hung in the sky, doing little to break up the darkness. They might as well have been in the middle of a rural field, instead of in the middle of a military base.

Together they trotted across the yard and slipped into the woods at the side of the road. The woods were so dark that Noah found himself slipping over rocks and fallen limbs. Sticks snapped under his feet. At every noise, Noah cringed.

"We sound like a pair of rhinos," Harley observed.

Noah stumbled to a stop. "This isn't going to work," he decided. He eased over to the edge of the woods. "We'll have to run along the side of the road," he said. "If we see anything, we can use the woods to hide."

Harley nodded. "That sounds better than tripping over tree roots."

As Noah jogged along the narrow road, he was surprised at how quiet the base really was. He had expected lots of jeeps and guys in uniform. So far, all they had seen was the empty road and the bare winter trees. In a way, the emptiness of the place only made it more frightening.

A light appeared through the branches ahead. Noah stopped and pulled out his map. He squinted at it in the dim light.

"I can't see well enough to be sure," he said. "But I think those are offices ahead."

"The commander's office," said Harley. "I've been there."

They moved on more slowly, hugging the edge of the woods as they approached the office. Small lights from each corner of the building shone down, but the lights didn't illuminate a very large area. There were no lights in the windows, and no sign of anyone around. The silence and stillness of the base was definitely starting to get on Noah's nerves.

"What do you think?" he asked. "Should we try to get inside?"

"I don't think so," whispered Harley. "I've been in there, and I didn't see anything. Unless you're ready to break into the commander's desk and start going through his things, we'd better skip it."

They moved into the woods to stay back from the lights and walked slowly around the office. Two more small square buildings followed, each of them apparently identical, and each of them dark. After that, there was another hundred yards of empty road before the shadowy form of a slender tower came into view.

The structure was as tall as a four-story building, but narrow. On its top level, a dim light shone through a ring of windows. A huge expanse of empty blacktop, glistening as though wet in the faint illumination, surrounded the tower. Further back were a pair of hangar-shaped buildings, each as big as a football stadium.

"I don't think this is on my map," said Noah.

"What part?"

"None of it." Noah folded the map and put it back in his pocket.

Harley pointed at the slender building. "I think that's a control tower for aircraft," she said. "Probably it's not on your map because the energy department didn't have any aircraft."

A shadow suddenly moved across the blacktop. Without a word, Noah and Harley dashed into the woods and hid among the trunks. The shadow passed again, sweeping quickly across the secret airfield.

"Someone's in the control tower," whispered Harley.

Noah looked up and saw a black silhouette moving behind the circle of windows. As the figure shifted, his shadow spread out over the ground like a passing giant.

"This runway must be a mile long," said Noah. "I can't even see the end." He licked his dry lips. "If we're going to go any further, we're going to have to cross it."

Harley crept over and stood close beside Noah. "If we go across there, someone's bound to see us."

She definitely had a point, but Noah wasn't ready to give up. He took a deep breath and stepped out from the trees. "I'll go first," he said. "If they catch me, you can run for the house."

Harley grabbed him by the arm. "No," she said. "You're not going without me."

Noah smiled at her, though he had no idea if she could see his pleased expression in the dark. "Come on then," he said. "I'll race you to the control tower."

He started across the blacktop at a sprint. His own breath in his ears sounded so loud that he was sure everyone within a mile could hear it. The glow from the moon, which had seemed so feeble before, now seemed like a spotlight shining down on him as he crossed the open space. At any moment, he expected sirens, lights, and a thousand guards. The shadow drifted over him, causing Noah to tense up so suddenly that he almost fell. Then, quicker than he had expected, he found himself pressed against the base of the control tower, hiding in the pool of darkness surrounding it.

Harley came running up a moment later. She bent over, hands on her knees. "It's not far to the buildings," she breathed. "Almost there."

Noah started to agree, but before he could speak, a horribly familiar gray fog rose up around him. A sharp, biting smell stung his nose. Murmuring voices grew into a buzz that filled his head.

"Almost done," said a flat voice.

Pale white faces appeared out of the gloom. Huge empty black eyes glared down at Noah as the faces circled around in a predatory pack.

"The trans-alpha patterns are coming through," said the voice. "It appears the implant is a success."

There was a sharp tug at Noah's arm. He spun around, tripped, and fell hard to the ground.

The faces around him vanished in a flash. He was back in the darkness beneath the control tower, laying on the cold blacktop.

"Are you all right?" whispered Harley, her voice filled with fear and concern.

Noah nodded slowly. "I think so," he told her hoarsely.

Harley reached down a hand and helped Noah

back to his feet. "I didn't mean to make you fall," she said. "But I couldn't get you out of it."

"It's okay," said Noah. He rubbed at his head. "Did I say anything this time?"

"Yeah," Harley replied. "You said trans-alpha again. And you said something about an implant."

The words echoed in Noah's mind, but already the memory of what he had heard in the dream was fading. He brushed dirt off his knees and started to walk around to the other side of the tower. "Come on," he said. "Let's run on across before the guy in the tower decides to come down for a coffee break."

They ran across the remaining gap and found themselves in an alley between the two huge metal buildings. Neither of the buildings had any windows or any visible doors. The walls were flat, featureless slabs of gray metal.

Noah ran his fingers over the smooth surface. "What do you think they are?"

"They look like hangers," whispered Harley.

Noah nodded. "That's what I thought, too. If what I read off the Net was right, there might be something a lot more interesting than planes inside. I wonder if that thing that followed us is in one of these."

"We won't know unless we get in," Harley said.

Noah walked on down the side of the building, looking for anything that might provide an entrance. Frustration gnawed at him. Right on the other side of either wall could be the answer to everything that was bothering him. If only he could find a way in.

He reached the corner and stared down the other

side. "Looks like there might be a door down at the far corner," Noah whispered.

He started down the width of the building. Suddenly Harley grabbed him painfully by the arm. Noah winced. "What's wrong?" he asked.

"Look," Harley said in a tense whisper.

Noah turned his head in the direction that Harley was staring, and his heart literally jumped in his chest.

Not a dozen yards beyond the plain metal hangers was a wonderland of silvery domes, slender spires, and giant metal mushrooms. Some of them were so small that no person could have squeezed inside. Others were as big as the high-school gym. The strange buildings, none shaped like anything Noah had ever seen, were clustered tightly together—so tightly that they became an almost incomprehensible mass of metal and ceramic. Pale green light played across the glittering surfaces of the buildings, but Noah couldn't see the light's source. For all he could tell, the buildings themselves were glowing.

"What *are* they?" Harley asked, her voice filled with awe.

Noah took a step toward the cluster of glowing buildings. "This has got to be the place," he said. "This is what this base is all about. If we're going to get any answers, they've got to be in there."

There was a road leading through another patch of forest toward the strange structures. Harley walked past Noah and started up the road. "There's something else up there," she noticed. "A fence of some kind."

They advanced cautiously. The fence was better than fifteen feet tall and topped with coils of gleaming razor wire. Ten feet beyond that was a second fence. The space in between was filled with harmless-looking sand, but Noah suspected it might be hiding a few nasty surprises.

"Be careful," Harley warned. She pointed up to a sign with red letters on a white background.

DANGER: 10,000 Volts
Contact will result
in immediate death

Noah took a step away from the fence. "Looks like they're serious about keeping people out of here."

Harley moved to the right. "There's a gate over here," she pointed out.

Noah joined her. There was a tiny box set beside the road with a small red light blinking on its face. "Maybe this will open the gate," he said.

"Maybe," Harley replied uncertainly. She bent down and peered at the box. "It looks like the security card box back at the house."

"They might notice if we open the gate, but I can't see how we'll get any further if we don't." Noah ran his finger over the slot. "You think your card will open this?"

"I doubt it," said Harley. She reached into the back pocket of her jeans and produced the small plastic rectangle. "But since we've come this far, I might as well give it a try."

She put the card into the thin slot and pushed it

in. The red light went out. A moment later a green light began to glow. "Looks like we have a winner," Harley said. She pulled out the card.

A blast of brilliance suddenly came from the trees at the side of the road, flooding the area of the gate with illumination brighter than noon sunlight. On the top of the fence, red lights pulsed and sirens shrieked.

"Run!" Noah shouted. "Into the woods!"

Harley was moving even before Noah finished speaking. She sprinted off the road and vanished in the darkness. Noah followed.

Blinded by the glaring lights, he ran into the trunk of a tree with bone-jarring force. Dizzily, he spun around, and then ran straight into a fence. For a moment he froze, sure that he was going to be fried by electricity, but no shock came.

He pulled himself away and turned around. Flashing red light slanted through the tangled tree branches. He clapped his hands over his ears to cut the din of the sirens.

"Harley!" Noah called.

He turned again and found himself facing the gate area. It was sliding slowly open. In the distance, headlights gleamed.

Noah ran. He could hear nothing now but the screech of sirens. He couldn't hear Harley. Even the noise of his own passage through the woods was lost in the shrieks of the sirens.

He came out on the edge of the runway and kept going. He was just past the control tower when the sirens abruptly stopped. With his ears ringing in the sudden silence, he heard a vehicle starting up some-where, and a distant shout.

Something shifted off to his left. Noah skidded to a halt and flattened himself against the base of the tower.

A dark shape loped along the side of the field, too distant to see clearly. A moment later, it vanished.

Noah thought the shape was Harley. But he couldn't be sure.

Behind him, someone shouted a command. A few seconds later, a second voice answered. They were close.

Noah charged straight across the blacktop, ignor-ing everything but the dark woods ahead. He heard another shout behind him, but he put his head down and ran as fast as he could.

Brilliant searchlights swept over him. He held up his hands to shield his eyes. Then he was back in the woods, crashing through the darkness. He charged on for a dozen yards, struggling to stay on his feet in the tangle of undergrowth and roots.

The small office buildings, which had only dim lights previously, were now topped by swinging spot-lights. The revolving lights cast crazy, spinning shad-ows through the forest. Noah stumbled, fell, and jumped back to his feet, crashing through the trees. Ten steps later, he fell again. Before he could pick himself up, a new light speared through the woods over his head.

Noah hugged the ground as a truck rolled slowly down the road. From the corner of his eye, he could see a soldier on top of the vehicle, turning a searchlight from side to side. The beam struck Noah and hesitated for a second. Then it moved on.

Warm blood trickled down the side of Noah's face as he climbed to his feet. The truck was driving slowly away down the road, its light swinging back and forth like the pendulum of a grandfather clock. After watching it for a moment, he realized that the light covered the woods to the left and right, but it didn't search behind the truck.

Noah dashed out of the woods and trotted along the side of the blacktop. He stayed about fifty yards behind the search vehicle, where he could keep it in sight, but also where he could still dash for the woods if it showed signs of turning around.

A minute later, the search beams were playing over the front of Harley's house. The truck stopped.

Noah left the road and ran back through the woods. He did his best to stay clear of the lights as he swung around and approached the house from behind. Then, using the building to shield himself, Noah ran up, grabbed the knob of the back door, and turned it. It was locked.

He thumped his hand against the door. "Harley," he called softly. There was no answer. He looked back at the woods. Harley was probably still out there somewhere, lost in the dark. Or maybe she had already been caught.

From the front of the house, he could hear serious, militaristic voices. A light shown through the gap between Harley's house and the next. Noah thumped the door again.

"Around here," called a gruff voice. "I think I saw something."

Noah pressed himself against the door. The light was moving, bobbing up and down as it drew closer. The shadow of an approaching figure spread across the grass.

The door behind Noah swung open and he fell inside. Before he could get to his feet, the door had been shut.

Harley knelt down beside him. "Are you all right?" she whispered.

"Ye . . . yeah," Noah replied through ragged gasps of breath. He held a hand up to his face and brought it back sticky with blood. "Or . . . maybe not."

Harley let out a strangled laugh. "We made it," she said. "I thought we were dead out there. But we made it."

There was a knock on the front door. From outside came a muffled shout.

Noah looked up into Harley's dark eyes. "Maybe not," he repeated.

ELEVEN

"Get up," Harley whispered. "You need to hide."

Noah climbed to his feet and stumbled across the dark kitchen, bumping into the counter. "Where?" he asked.

Harley bit her lip and looked around quickly. "The bedroom," she said. "Come on."

She grabbed Noah's hand and dragged him through the house. By the time they reached the bedroom, the knocking at the door had turned into pounding.

"Just a minute!" Harley shouted, trying to sound annoyed. "I'm *coming!*"

She pulled the black sweater over her head and slid out of her jeans. Even in the dim light she could see Noah looking at her with wide eyes. "Do you *mind?*" Harley snapped. Noah quickly turned his head.

Harley snatched up a robe from the chair beside the bed. "Get out of sight," she told him. "Maybe we'll get lucky."

The pounding at her door grew louder. "Ms. Davisidaro!" called a voice. "Are you in there?"

"I said, I'm coming!"

Harley was halfway to the door when she spotted both the pistol and the journals she had taken from her father's coat lying on the coffee table. She quickly backtracked and grabbed them. Harley dropped them all into the deep pocket of her robe. Then she ran over to the door.

She eased open the door to find Colonel Braddock standing on her porch. Next to him was the guard who had held the clipboard when Harley first arrived at the base. This time he didn't have a clipboard. He had a gun.

"What's going on?" Harley asked. She did her best to sound sleepy. "Do you know what *time* it is?"

The base commander leaned past her and looked into the living room. "We've had a security breach," he said brusquely. "We need to inspect your residence."

"Okay," Harley agreed. "I mean, if you have to." She held a hand over her face, stifling a pretend yawn. "But I thought no one can get in these places without a pass card."

The commander stepped past her and stood in the center of the living room. "They can't," he replied.

Harley crossed her arms over her chest. "Well, then," she said. "You don't need to search here. I've got my pass card and I haven't let anyone in."

Two more guards approached the porch. "Commander, we've had a report of activity near the front gate."

"*Blast* it," Braddock swore. "All right. I'll be right there." He looked down at Harley. "You keep your doors closed, Ms. Davisidaro. Do you understand?"

"Yes, sir," said Harley.

The commander marched out of the house. The guards stared at Harley for a moment, and she got the distinct impression that they wanted to do more than stare. But after a moment, they turned and followed their commander.

Harley slammed the door shut and leaned against it. She heard the sound of the truck starting up outside and moving away toward the main gate.

Noah emerged from the bedroom and peeked around the corner. "They gone?"

Harley nodded. "As far as I know." She stepped away from the door. "I don't know if they believed me. They might be back."

Noah ran his fingers through his floppy blond hair and shook his head. "We were there," he said. "We were right there. Next time, we'll get inside. And then—"

"Hold it," Harley interrupted. A warm flush of anger surged over her skin. "We almost got killed out there. You *can't* want to do it again."

"Well, not right away," Noah replied defensively. "But we've got to find out what's really going on, don't we?"

Harley stared into his face and shook her head. "I want my father back worse than anything," she said, "but getting myself killed is not going to get him back."

Noah looked down and was silent for a moment. Then he said in a small voice, "I've got to know what's going on. I can't live with these dreams for another week. I just *can't*."

"But I don't know what to do," Harley protested softly. Suddenly she felt very, very tired. She walked over to the end of the couch and collapsed onto the cushions. "I just don't know what we should do."

Noah came over and sat down beside her. A thin line of blood still trickled from a cut on his forehead, but he didn't seem to notice. "I think I should go now."

Harley looked at him for a moment. Then she shook her head. "It's too late to go anywhere." She pushed her hair back from her face and adjusted the front of her robe. "You'll have to stay the rest of the night," she decided. "They'll be suspicious if I try to leave now."

"All right," Noah agreed. He dabbed at the cut on his head. "I guess I'll go clean up a little." He stood and took a step toward the bathroom.

"You have your choice," Harley said firmly, standing up to face him. "You can stay in my father's bedroom, or you can have the couch."

Noah turned to look at her over his shoulder. There was a slight look of disappointment on his face. "I guess I'll take the bed," he replied. "But not right now. I'm too keyed up to sleep."

"Good," said a new voice. "Then you can listen to me."

Harley jumped to her feet and whirled around, expecting to see the base commander and a squad of soldiers with guns. What she found instead was a man sitting on the couch. He was a thin man, with a dark suit and a hat that made him look like he had stepped out of an old detective film from the 1940s.

Noah ran toward the door, but the man held up a hand. "Please don't leave, Mr. Templer. I need to speak with both of you." His voice was a rattling whisper, like gravel going down a pipe.

"Who are you?" demanded Harley.

The man fished in the pocket of his suit and came out with a black ballpoint pen. "My name is Cain," he said in his rasping voice. "Ian Cain."

"How did you get in here?" Harley glanced at the kitchen counter, checking to see if there was a knife or anything else that might serve as a weapon.

Cain began rhythmically clicking the retractable point of the pen. "Let's just say that's one of my little secrets," he replied.

"I don't appreciate having people break into my house at two in the morning," Harley told him. She realized that the front of her robe had begun to come open and tugged it firmly closed.

"Really?" Cain looked at her and gave a mild smile. "I don't appreciate having people break into my home at any time of the day. However, in this case I had no choice."

"Are you from the base?"

Cain shrugged. He pressed the end of the pen again—*click, click—click, click*.

"Not really," he said finally, absentmindedly twirling the pen in his fingers. He reached into his coat again, and this time he produced a badge with his own picture on one side and the letters FBI on the other. He held the badge toward them for a moment. Then he flipped it closed and shoved it back into his pocket.

Noah took a step forward. "What would the FBI be doing on a military base?" he asked.

Cain gave a soft chuckle. "Who told you this was a military base?"

"Of *course* it's a military base," Harley said impatiently. "What else could it be?"

"This facility is under the control of Unit 17," said Cain. He clicked the pen again, as though the sound was punctuation. "And Unit 17 is not exactly a military organization."

Harley shook her head. "My father always works for the military."

"I'm afraid you are mistaken." Cain stood up. He was taller than Harley had thought, taller even than Noah, with a narrow face and a long lantern jaw. His eyes were set so deep in his face that it was impossible to tell their color. His black suit fit him well. Even at a glance, Harley could tell that it was something that had been carefully tailored to fit only Cain, not something from the rack at a department store.

"What do you know about this place?" Noah asked.

Cain walked slowly across the room and lifted one of the slats in the blinds. "You two caused quite a stir tonight," he said. He leaned down and peeked through the opening. "Did you make a habit of disturbing ants' nests when you were younger?"

Harley felt a jolt of alarm at Cain's mocking tone. "We haven't done anything."

Cain chuckled again. "Don't worry, I'm not here to arrest you. I've got more important goals in mind."

Noah took a step closer to Cain. "You said this place wasn't a military base," he said. "Then what is it?"

"Something else," Cain replied. He released the blind and leaned back against the wall. "Something quite different." He resumed pressing his thumb down on the end of the pen—*click, click—click, click—click, click—*

127

The agent's casual manner and his rhythmic pen clicking began to irritate Harley. "Can you *stop* that?" she asked. "That sound really gets on my nerves."

Cain shrugged. He slid the pen back into his pocket. Then he looked at Harley. "Now," he said, "about your father."

A mixture of hope and fear tightened Harley's throat. "What about him?"

"I know you haven't seen him in two days," said Cain. "I know they told you he was away. But at this point my sources indicate that your father never left this base."

"He's here?" Harley took a step forward, and then stopped. "Why should I believe a word you say?"

"Don't," Cain answered calmly. "I certainly would never recommend trusting in the kindness of strangers. But has anyone else bothered to offer you information about your father?"

"No," Harley admitted. "So you think he's here?"

"That I don't know," Cain replied. He pulled the black pen from his pocket, looked at it for a moment, then put it back. "He's not dead, we know that much. But that's all we know."

Harley felt her knees go soft, and she leaned against the dining table to keep from falling to the floor. She hadn't wanted to admit to herself that her father *could* be dead, but that fear had been tormenting her all along. Just finding out he was alive was worth everything they had been through that night. Her relief was so strong, she even started to feel a little more warmly toward Cain.

"Will you get him out?" she asked.

Cain nodded. "If it's possible." He paced back across the room. "First I need to gather a little information."

Noah folded his arms. "What information?" he asked. "Why are you really here?"

"As I said," replied Cain, "to collect information."

"What *kind* of information?" Noah shot back curtly.

Harley glanced at Noah, surprised momentarily by his suspicious rudeness, since she was feeling nothing but relief that her father wasn't dead. Noah's guarded expression and narrowed eyes reminded her that they really knew nothing about Cain. She and Noah had to be extremely careful about trusting anything he said. "Yeah," she told Cain. "It's time for you to get specific."

"Ah." Cain absently reached into his pocket and took out the pen again. Then he glanced at Harley and tried to slide it back into his pocket, missing on the first attempt. Finally, the black pen was once again secure in his suit jacket pocket. "Nervous tic," he growled. He raised his glance from where the pen rested in his pocket and looked over at Noah. "This is a highly unusual situation. Unit 17 tends to operate somewhat outside normal procedures. In this case, they may have gone too far outside the limits."

"But why are *you* here?" asked Harley. Cain opened his mouth to answer, but Harley cut him off. "I don't mean why are you here on the base," she clarified. "I mean, why are you here in my living room?"

"Now we're coming to the heart of things," Cain

said approvingly. "I'm in your living room because I need your help."

Harley shook her head. "I don't see what we can do."

"You did well enough tonight," Cain pointed out.

Harley bit her lip. He probably already knew about their activities that night—he did seem to have an uncanny knowledge of *everything*—but Harley wasn't about to make it easy for him if he was just guessing. "I don't know what you're talking about," she said.

Cain strolled around the couch. "I'm talking about your little exploits around the base."

"What?" Harley asked, feigning innocence.

"Come now," said Cain. "I'm not stupid and neither are you. Though you *are* extremely lucky."

"Lucky?" asked Noah with a grim laugh. "I don't *feel* all that lucky."

"I mean, simply, that were it not for my intervention, you'd be resting in a holding cell." Cain turned his head slightly and flashed a thin smile. "Or you might be dead."

"Intervention," Harley said carefully. Her nerves were jangling. All the positive feelings she'd had toward Cain when he'd told her that her father was still alive had evaporated. He was now definitely starting to creep her out.

"You should be very glad of my help," Cain added. "If I hadn't diddled with the base computer systems, they'd know that the pass card inserted into the inner gate was yours."

"How did you know about—" Harley began.

Noah walked over to Harley and leaned in close

to her ear. "Careful. Don't tell him anything," he whispered.

Harley looked across the room at Cain. "I'm being as careful as I can," she replied through gritted teeth. "But I think he already knows everything."

"You should listen to her," Cain told Noah with an easy smile. "She's a very smart young woman." The agent crossed the carpeted floor and stopped only an arm's length in front of Harley and Noah. "She's changed schools six times in seven years," he said, "but still maintains a three-point-two GPA. You, Mr. Templer, have also done well over the years, though of late you have experienced difficulty."

Close up, Cain was younger than Harley had first thought. His hat, his dark suit, and his formal way of talking made Cain seem older than Harley's father, but now that she could see his face clearly, he looked no more than twenty-five.

"Great," said Noah. "You seem to know all about us. How about telling us something that we don't know?" There was an edge of anger in his voice.

Cain reached up and tipped his hat back from his face, revealing a high forehead and a lock of brown hair. "Fair enough," he said. "Do you understand what a black project is?"

"Something the government is doing that they don't want us to know anything about," Noah answered.

Cain nodded. "As they say, that's close enough for government work. Such projects tend to get out of control if they are not properly supervised. This base is just such a project." He looked hard at Noah. "A project which deals with some . . . very special technology, Mr. Templer."

"Alien technology," said Noah. The anger evaporated out of his face. "It's really here."

"You'll understand if I don't get any more specific," Cain said. "There are restrictions on what I can say." He shrugged. "The most important thing is that this project has gone disturbingly off the rails. I'm here to see that things are made right."

"We'll help," Noah said eagerly.

Harley put her hand on his shoulder. "Wait," she said. She looked at Cain. "Why should we help? He's told us nothing so far, really."

Cain looked around at her, an annoyed frown fixed over his thin face. "I explained—"

Harley shook her head. "You didn't explain anything. You told us you want information. But there's a big difference between you wanting the information and me getting it for you."

"I don't suppose love of country is enough to compel you?" Cain asked. His voice was heavy with sarcasm.

"I love my country as much as anyone," Harley replied evenly. "But how do I know you aren't the one who's trying to hurt it?"

Cain nodded. "I see. You need proof that I'm on the side of the angels." He turned and began to walk around the living room in slow circles. "I'm not sure what I can say to convince you that my motives are pure," he said. "What do you want?"

"My father," Harley answered immediately.

"He's not mine to provide," Cain said. "However,

I can assure you, should you gather the information I require, we will take swift action."

Harley thought about it for a moment, and then shook her head. "That's not much of a promise," she said. "I want more than that."

"I don't have more to give you," Cain replied. "Simply, you're just going to have to trust me. Although there's no reason you should." He stopped and his head swung from Harley to Noah. "However, I can also provide some information of interest to Mr. Templer."

"More nonsense about aliens?" asked Harley.

Noah looked at her with a hurt expression. "How can you say it's nonsense?" he asked. "You saw that base tonight."

"I saw it," Harley replied. "Look, I admit it was strange, but that doesn't mean it had anything to do with aliens."

"This has nothing to do with aliens," said Cain. "Though it does have to do with this base." He waited until both Harley and Noah had turned their attention back to him before he went on. "There is a girl," he said, tapping his fingertips together in front of his chest in a gesture of prayer. "A certain Caroline Crewson."

"Is she here?" Noah asked quickly.

Cain nodded. "Almost certainly. And if you want answers to your recent . . . *problems*, this base is the only place for you to look."

"So," Noah said. "Let me get this straight. We're talking about *trading* information, right? We go into the base and find out what you need to know, and in return, Harley gets her father back, we rescue Caroline, and I get my . . . *answers*. Does that sum it up?"

"Rather marvelously," Cain replied.

Noah turned to Harley. "We've got to help. We have to help get them out—your father and Caroline. And I've got to find out if I'm crazy or not."

Harley pressed her lips together. She wanted to believe Cain. She wanted to believe that if she did what the agent wanted, her father would be back safe and sound. Harley glanced over at Noah. He was staring at her with an expectant expression on his face, waiting for her to make the final decision. She sighed. Cain didn't *feel* right to her, but he was the only lead they had—and she had to move forward, she had to take action toward finding her father. "I guess we don't have any choice," she said reluctantly. She looked up at the tall agent. "What is it you want?"

Cain smiled at her. It was a very unconvincing smile. "All I want is a repeat of tonight's performance. You go in. You observe. You get out." He snapped his fingers. "Simple as that."

"How can we observe anything?" asked Harley. "We can't get inside. We found that out tonight."

"Ah," said Cain. "This time, I'll provide more direct assistance." He reached into his jacket and produced a small card. It was the same size as Harley's pass card, but this one was jet black on both sides. "You'll find that this card has access to most locations on the base."

Harley took the card from Cain's fingers. Only after she was holding it did she notice how badly her hand was trembling. "We might be killed," she said softly.

"If you don't do this," said Cain calmly, "you will almost certainly be killed. And quite soon."

Harley's hand dropped into the pocket of her robe and she felt the comforting weight of the pistol beside her father's journals. "Is that a threat?"

"Far from it," said Cain. "I'm working exceptionally hard to keep you alive." A low trilling sound suddenly sounded.

"Excuse me," Cain said. From some hidden recess of his suit, he produced a small cellular phone and flipped it open. "Yes?" he asked into the mouthpiece. There was a pause, then Cain added, "I see." He closed the phone and slid it back into his pocket.

"I have to run," he told Harley and Noah. "I'll contact you tomorrow." He turned and started across the room, bumping gently into Harley as he passed her.

Cain nodded his head when he reached the front door. "We'll talk later," he told them. Then he opened the door, slipped out, and closed it quietly behind him.

Harley ran across the room and grabbed the edge of the blinds. The emergency lights were still shining on the street outside, casting harsh shadows and filling the night with hard white light.

But there was no sign of Cain.

"That guy totally freaks me out," she told Noah. "He makes me feel . . . *itchy*."

"I know exactly what you mean," Noah replied. "But who else can help? At least he's not trying to kill us."

"That's true," Harley said with a sigh. Again, she slipped her hand into her robe pocket to feel the comforting weight of the pistol. She closed her hand around its muzzle, which was cold in her grip. Then, with a gasp, she released the pistol and began digging frantically in her pocket.

"What's the matter?" Noah asked.

Harley stopped her search and faced him. "My father's journals," she said. "They're gone."

TWELVE

Even though it was chilly outside, the inside of the trunk quickly became stifling.

Noah lay with his knee smashed up against the spare tire and a flashlight wedged under his ribs. Something sharp was digging into his shin, but it was too dark to figure out what it was. Through the trunk lid he could hear the muffled sound of Harley talking with the guards. The conversation seemed to be going on forever.

Finally a door slammed and the car began to move. A few minutes later it stopped again. There was a clatter of keys, and the trunk swung open.

"All out for Stone Harbor," Harley called.

Noah blinked at the sunlight and unfolded himself. With Harley's help, he got out of the trunk and stepped down onto the grass at the side of the road. "I don't think I can ride in there anymore. I'm starting to get tread marks on my face."

"Then you better figure out another way in," said Harley. "That is, unless you're giving up on helping Cain."

"No," said Noah. "We have to help Cain."

Harley sighed. "How can we trust him? He stole my father's journals! And what has he really told us?"

Noah climbed into the passenger seat. "Say we *don't* listen to Cain," he proposed. "What then?"

Harley shrugged. "We keep looking on our own."

137

"Where?" Noah asked. "We know your father and Caroline are both on the base."

"Wrong," said Harley. "We know that Cain *says* they're on the base. He could be telling us that just to get us to do his dirty work. He's using us." She stopped at a stop sign and turned to face Noah. "I want my dad back. That's all that matters to me right now."

"Right," said Noah. "So we should help Cain."

"But what if helping Cain is the worst thing we can do? We'll be risking our lives if we go back in there." Harley's black eyes glittered and her voice grew husky. "I'll do it, though, no matter what the risk, just as long as it doesn't get my dad killed."

Noah took a deep breath. "I have to go back in there," he said. "*Have to*. I have to find out where the dreams are coming from. I just *know* there's a connection."

"Is finding out about the dreams worth your life?" Harley asked.

Noah put his hands over his face. "I'm not crazy," he said. "Not yet, anyway. But if I don't find out what's going on, I think it may drive me crazy."

"Yeah, well, you won't get there far ahead of me," Harley said softly. She slowed the car as they reached Stone Harbor. "I think I may have a way we can check on Mr. Ian Cain."

"How's that?"

Instead of answering, Harley turned the car to the left and drove into a neighborhood of old, but well-cared-for homes. A moment later she pulled into the driveway of a two-story wooden house with fresh blue paint and an old gray slate roof.

"Dee's house," said Noah. "You sure about this?"

Harley opened her door. "Come on. Let's see who's home."

Dee had opened the front door before Noah could get out of the car. "Well, look at you two," Dee joked. "One date and you're inseparable."

"Hi, Dee," said Harley. "I was hoping to talk to your dad."

Dee threw her head back and pressed her arm to her forehead. "Everyone only wants to see my father," she said. "No one loves me for myself." She looked down, grinned, and opened the door. "Come on in. He's still working on breakfast."

Inside the house, they found Dee's father sitting by a plate of French toast and bacon. Mr. Janes got to his feet as they came through the door. "Well, hello, Noah. Ms. Davisidaro. I didn't know you two were friends."

"Another part of the plot to break my heart," said Dee.

Her father smiled. "I'm sure. Mrs. Janes has gone off to sell a house, but she left plenty of food behind. Sit down and have something to eat."

Noah wasn't particularly hungry, but he was too tired to resist the offer to sit. He took a chair at the side of the table. Harley sat down by his side.

Sitting there in Dee's kitchen, Noah felt like he had come up from a trip deep under the ocean, or escaped from some dark cave. Everything in the room seemed so normal. With the smell of bacon in the air and the sun shining through the window, everything that had happened the night before seemed like a bad dream.

Noah laughed. "Dreams."

Dee's father looked at him across the table. "What's that, Noah?"

Noah realized he had spoken aloud. He felt his face flush with embarrassment. "Nothing," he said. "I'm just tired. Is Caroline still missing?"

Mr. Janes nodded. "So, you want to talk about it?" The police chief's face stayed as friendly as ever, but his voice had an undertone of something more serious.

"There's nothing to tell," Noah said. "I saw Caroline at the library on Wednesday afternoon. I haven't seen her since then."

"Mrs. Tich, the librarian, says you did more than *see* Caroline." Dee's father put down his fork and leaned toward Noah. "She says you two had something of a fight."

"We talked," Noah replied. "That's all."

"I see." Mr. Janes looked at Noah for a long moment. Then he picked up his fork. "If you remember anything else, you'll be sure to tell me, right?"

Noah nodded. One part of the tightness in his stomach relaxed a notch. "Sure."

"What about my dad?" Harley asked. "I was hoping you might have found out something."

Dee's father rubbed his chin. "I did find something," he said. "But I'm not sure I can tell you what it means. Wait here." He left the table and went into another room. When he came back a moment later, he had a small stack of papers in his hand. He took the top page and handed it to Harley. "Here, take a look at this."

Noah leaned in to read over her shoulder. The paper

was topped with a series of numbers and small codes. Right below that was the name "Franklin Davisidaro." It was followed by a birth date, a list of college degrees, and even a record of a pair of traffic tickets.

"This is my dad," said Harley. "But there's not much there."

"Think so?" Dee's father handed over the second sheet. "Take a look at this one."

The second page was also headed by a cluster of numbers, and then by Harley's father's name. But below that was nothing.

"I don't understand," said Harley. "What does it mean?"

Dee's father tapped his finger against the sheet that had more information. "I ran this one right after I talked to you on Friday."

"What about the blank page?" asked Noah.

"That's the one I ran last night." Dee's father took the paper back, looked at it, and shook his head. "There's nothing in there now. All the information about Frank Davisidaro has been erased."

Harley looked from Mr. Janes to Noah and back again. There was more fear in her brown eyes than Noah had ever seen before. "How can that be?" she asked, her voice trembling.

"I don't know," said Mr. Janes. "This information base draws on records from universities, the military, motor vehicle licensing, even the phone company. And look at this." He held up the nearly blank page. "The system is supposed to record every time someone makes a data request on a subject. But even the search I ran on Friday is gone."

Noah stared at the white paper. "A worm," he said softly.

"What?" Harley asked.

"A computer worm," Noah replied. "It's a program that can move from system to system. If you program it right, it can eat just the data you want out of every system on the Net. This one must have been programmed to find and erase files that had anything to do with Harley's father."

Harley's olive skin went pale. "If they're erasing the files, they don't expect him to come back, do they?"

Noah laid his hand over hers. "We don't know that, Harley."

"Sure," Harley said quietly. "Sure we do."

Dee came over and put an arm around Harley's shoulder. "You look tired," she said. "You want to go rest for a while?"

Harley shook her head and sat up very straight in her chair. "No," she said. "There's too much to do." She turned and looked at Dee's father. "Does your computer connect to the FBI?"

The trooper nodded. "It does. As long as you don't want anything too fancy."

"I want to see if you can find an agent for me," said Harley. "An agent named Ian Cain."

Dee's father frowned so hard that lines grew down the length of his face. "Before I look for this Cain guy, could you at least give me a hint what this is all about?"

"Agent Cain contacted me and said he knew something about my father," Harley told Mr. Janes. "But I'm not sure he's for real."

Noah admired the way that Harley was able to tell what essentially was the truth, without giving away anything about their midnight run through the base. He doubted he could have done half as well.

"I'll check him out," Dee's father promised. "I can't tell you what he knows, but at least we'll see if he's a real agent."

Dee got out a pair of plates and loaded them with French toast and crisp bacon. "Here," she said. "You should never worry on an empty stomach."

As soon as the plate landed in front of Noah, he realized that he was hungry after all. He made three thick slices of bread disappear before coming up for air. Even Harley managed to take a few bites of her food.

Mr. Janes left the house, saying that he was going to his office to check his computer. Dee sat down across the kitchen table from Harley and Noah. She propped her head in her hands and looked from Noah to Harley and back again.

"It's too late, isn't it?" Dee asked.

Noah raised his eyebrows. "Too late for what?"

"Too late for me," Dee replied. "Too late for Caroline. Too late for all the other girls at school." She nodded toward Harley. "Tell me I'm wrong."

Noah opened his mouth and started to do just that. There was nothing going on between himself and Harley. They hadn't even kissed. In fact, it was hard to think of a conversation where they had done much more than argue. For all that, Noah found himself unable to disagree with Dee.

"I . . ." Noah closed his eyes momentarily. "I don't know."

Harley just shrugged.

Dee leaned away from the table. "When are you two going to tell me what's really going on?"

Noah glanced over at Harley. "What makes you think anything's going on?"

Dee rolled her eyes. "Please. What do you think I am, an adult? I know a good lie when I hear one. Now give."

"I don't think we can." Noah grimaced. "Not yet."

"Why not?" Dee asked with a frown. "You think I can't keep a secret?"

"Well . . ."

Dee's eyes narrowed into slits. "All right," she said. "Don't tell me. But when this thing is over, I get a full report."

"That's a deal," agreed Noah. He caught sight of a clock at the end of the counter. "We're going to have to get moving," he said. "I've got to pick up my car and let my parents know I'm still alive."

"And don't forget there's a big algebra test on Monday," said Dee. She wrinkled her nose. "I know, I know, it sounds lame. But if you live through the weekend, wouldn't you like to be prepared for class?"

Noah and Harley headed for the door. Dee reached out and took Harley's wrist. "Why don't you come over here and stay for a while?" she said. "We've got an extra room, and I know my parents would be happy to have you."

"I'll think about it," Harley said, her voice betraying her exhaustion. "Maybe when this thing is over."

"You better hope it's over soon," said Dee. "Both

of you look like refugees from a sleep deprivation experiment."

Noah rubbed his eyes. Now that he had eaten, a few days of sleep did seem like the best thing to do. They climbed into Harley's car and headed back through town.

"Where did you leave your car?" asked Harley.

"Down by Lake Malone," Noah replied. "In case anyone saw it, I wanted my camping story to hold up. So I parked out there and ran back in to meet you." He pointed to the west. "It's about five miles out of town."

Harley drove on through the business district, across a valley filled with farmer's fields, and up into more rolling wooded hills. "How is Cain going to find us?" she said as they topped a long hill. "He didn't say where we were supposed to meet him."

"I don't know," said Noah. "How did he find us in the first place?"

A horn sounded behind them. Noah twisted around in his seat and saw a dark car right on their rear bumper. "Looks like this guy's in a big hurry," he said grumpily.

"I'll be happy to let him pass," Harley replied. "But there's nowhere to pull over."

Noah glanced out his side window. Harley was right. The shoulder of the road was only a few feet wide. Beyond that, the hill angled down steeply. But when he looked back, he saw that the car behind them had already edged out into the left lane and was moving up along their side.

"Better slow down," Noah warned. "It looks like this guy isn't going to wait."

Harley eased off the gas. The dark car began to slide past.

When the nose of the car had reached the front seat, Noah realized that he had seen the car before.

On a dark street.

Trying to run him down.

"Harley! Watch out for—"

Before he could finish his statement, there was a crash of metal. Harley fought with the wheel as they were pushed off to the right. The car slammed into them again and they were forced into the gravel at the side of the road. "Are they *crazy?*" she cried.

The black car was almost even with them now. Noah looked over and saw the shadowy forms of three figures behind deeply tinted glass. The car swerved right to strike them again.

This time Harley threw her wheel to the left and smashed into the other car in a gut-wrenching blow. Metal screeched and a network of cracks appeared in the windshield. The black car moved away.

"There's a road coming up on the right," Noah said urgently. "If you can hold on till then, we can pull over."

Harley nodded. "I can try."

They went on another ten seconds running side by side with the black car. Noah was beginning to think they might actually make it when the passenger-side window of the black car slid down. A hand emerged. In it was a rod of dull gray metal.

There was a flash of brilliant white light.

Instantly Noah was back in the dark room, surrounded by white faces and the murmur of some

146

alien tongue. He could smell the sharp odor of antiseptic. He could feel a cold metal table under his back.

"All right," said a cold, emotionless voice. "Let's get prepared."

There was a rattle. From the corner of his eye, Noah saw a tray of surgical instruments being pushed up to the side of the table. A gloved hand reached down and selected a curved scalpel.

"The insertion will be simple," said the voice. The scalpel moved up, out of Noah's view. He felt cold pressure on his back, directly beneath his right shoulder blade.

"Get ready to test reception."

A thunderous crash reverberated around him. The faces vanished, and with them the knife, the table, and even the sharp, bitter smell.

Only the darkness remained.

THIRTEEN

There was a sudden flood of light, like a thousand flashbulbs all going off at once.

For a moment, Harley was overwhelmed by memories. She was a child running across a deep green lawn. Her mother was there, smiling at her, reaching out. Harley felt cool grass under her bare feet.

Then there was a crash from the left. The image of Harley's mother shattered like a broken mirror.

Harley looked around to see the dark sedan still at her side. With one hand on the wheel, she reached for her bag. Her fingers moved across a billfold, some papers, and then the cold weight of the revolver. Harley grabbed the pistol and dragged it free.

The sedan crashed into the side of her car again.

Harley fought with the wheel. She raised the revolver and turned to the left.

Another jarring collision forced her off the road on the right. Gravel hissed under the tires as the car left the blacktop.

Harley pointed the gun at the window of the sedan. "Stop!" she screamed. "Stop now!"

The sedan swung in and delivered a final blow, driving Harley completely off the road. For a moment, her car seemed to hover, with two wheels still bumping along the road and two hanging in the air. Then the car tilted right. And down.

Harley's view blurred as the car plummeted over

the hill and began to roll down the steep slope. Trees whipped by on the left and right. The world spun head over heels. The seat belt dug into Harley's shoulder as she was slammed up and down. From somewhere there was a sharp scream. It took Harley several seconds to realize it was coming from her mouth.

The car crashed against a stump, spun around, and slid down the hill backward. They struck another obstacle. Harley's head was thrown back against the seat so fast that stars danced in front of her eyes. Finally, when the car seemed close to stopping, it plowed into a tree, tipped onto its side, and then rolled completely over to rest on its roof.

There was a soft creak and groan of metal. Mud bubbled up around the cracked windshield. Then there was nothing to disturb the silence but Harley's tortured breathing.

She was upside down, but nothing seemed to be broken. The pistol was still in her right hand, held so tightly that her whole arm trembled. At some point, she thought she had pulled the trigger, but if the gun had fired, she hadn't noticed it. Maybe it wasn't even loaded.

Harley dropped the gun and fumbled for the seat belt latch. It came free with a pop, spilling her painfully against the steering wheel. She twisted around and saw Noah.

He was still dangling in his seat belt and shoulder harness. His eyes were closed and his face was unnaturally pale.

"Noah?" Harley asked anxiously. "Noah, can you

hear me?" She stretched to put her hand against his neck. His skin felt cool and damp, but she could feel the pulse of Noah's blood under her trembling hand. Harley let out a relieved breath.

Noah murmured something.

"Noah?" Harley asked again. "Are you all right?"

"Get prepared," Noah said. His voice was dead flat—the voice of his dreams.

Harley took hold of his sleeve and pulled his arm back and forth. "Come on, Noah. Wake up!"

"The insertion will be simple," said Noah. His arm flopped bonelessly in Harley's grip.

Harley bit her lip. Noah had always come out of the dreams when she shook him, but this time he seemed locked inside. Maybe it had something to do with the car wreck. He might be really hurt.

"Get ready to test reception," Noah mumbled. He jerked suddenly, swinging back and forth in his harness.

Harley let go of his arm. She thought about unlocking Noah's belt and pulling him from the car, but she had no idea how badly he was injured. Moving him might kill him. "Hold on," she said. "I'm going to go get some help."

Turned on its top, the car seemed horribly small and confining. Harley cracked down the window on her door, letting in a slurry of mud and water. She squirmed through the muck, emerging into a world of swampy weeds.

From the outside, the car was an almost invisible lump in a heap of brush and fallen saplings. Dark red transmission fluid leaked from the car like blood.

Harley raised her head and followed the path they had taken down the slope with her gaze. Their trail was well marked by uprooted shrubs and gouged earth.

She wadded across the swampy ground and started up the slope. If she was going to find help, her best chance was to head back to the highway.

Of course, the people that had tried to kill them were also on the highway. Harley hesitated, looking up the hill. She saw no one and heard nothing. It seemed as though the dark sedan and those inside it had moved on.

The hill was steep and the ground was damp. At two spots Harley was forced to get down on her hands and knees to make progress. At other places she had to pull herself up by grabbing onto shrubs and stunted pine trees. By the time she reached the road, she felt as though she had scaled Mount Everest.

There was no one in sight on the highway. Harley stood there for several minutes, shivering in the cold wind. Her wet and muddy shirt clung to her, adding to her misery. Though it had been before noon when they left Dee's house, hours seemed to have passed. The sun was already dipping toward the horizon. Night wasn't far away.

Harley looked down the slope. From the edge of the road, she could just make out one corner of the wrecked car. Noah had not come out. "Noah!" she shouted. "Noah! Are you awake?" There was no reply.

It was three or four miles back to town. The park where Noah had left his car was closer, but Harley had never been there. She had no idea if the place would even have a phone. Shivering against the cold and still dripping muddy water, Harley turned toward Stone Harbor and started walking.

She had gone only a few hundred yards when she heard an approaching car. Harley tensed. She wondered if it was the black sedan coming back to finish them off.

A pickup truck appeared around the corner. Harley smiled in relief. She held up her arms and waved them back and forth. "Help!" she called. "We need help!"

The truck swerved to move around her. Without slowing, it sped on over the next hill and out of sight.

Harley put her hands on her hips and stared after it. "Jerk!" she shouted.

A car horn honked at her back. Harley jumped and spun around. An off-white compact car stood so close behind her that she could have reached out to touch the hood.

A woman leaned out the window. "You look like you're in trouble," she said.

It took Harley a moment to recognize the woman. She took a step around the corner of the car. "Coach Rocklin?"

The track coach opened her door and stepped out. "Harley? Is that you?" She ran over to Harley, her face tight with worry. "What happened? How did you end up out here?"

"There was a car. It ran us . . ." Harley stopped and pushed muddy hair away from her face. "An accident," she said. "I ran off the road."

Coach Rocklin raised her hand and wiped it across Harley's cheek. "Are you all right?"

Harley nodded. "I'm fine," she replied. She looked over her shoulder. "But Noah Templer's back there. He's still in the car and I think he might be hurt."

"Noah?" said the coach. "Come on. My house is only a minute from here. We'll go there and call 911."

"Maybe I should wait here to show them the right spot," suggested Harley.

Coach Rocklin shook her head. "Nonsense. You're soaking wet. If you stay out here much longer they'll be taking you to the hospital for exposure. You come with me."

Harley followed her back to the car and climbed inside. The track coach dropped into the driver's seat and turned the car around in the road.

"Don't worry," she said. "The rescue unit will be out here in a snap. They'll take care of Noah."

"I hope so." Harley looked down at her legs. "I'm getting mud all over your car."

"Don't worry about that, either," Coach Rocklin assured her. "It's an old car."

They turned off onto a gravel drive and bumped along between an apple orchard on one side and fields on the other. It was probably a pretty place in the summer, but at the moment the leafless trees were like rows of dark scarecrows.

Coach Rocklin's house was an old two-story farmhouse. A handful of chickens went fluttering as she pulled up into the front yard. "Come on in," she said as she opened her door. "I'll call the emergency services."

Harley followed her up the steps and into the house. Track trophies covered every shelf in the front room. Coach Rocklin disappeared into the back, and then returned with a cup of coffee. "I wouldn't usually give this to a student," she said. "But you need to warm up. Drink it down."

Harley took the cup gratefully. The smell alone was enough to make her feel better. "Did you call 911?"

The track coach nodded. "They're on their way," she said. "You have a seat. I'm going to call Noah's parents and let them know what's going on. Then you and I will go make sure the crew gets to the right place."

"Okay." Harley sat down on the couch, cradling the warm coffee in her hands. "I'm ready whenever you are."

Coach Rocklin gave her a smile. "I'm sure Noah's fine," she said. "Just wait and see." She went back down the hall.

For a minute or more, Harley sat without moving. It was so nice to be sitting on the soft couch in the warm house. She felt as though she could stay there for a week.

Harley lifted coffee to her lips to take a sip, but the cup slipped from her tired hand. Hot coffee spilled across her legs and onto the floor.

Harley jumped to her feet and brushed the coffee away. She picked up the cup and went in search of a towel.

There was a kitchen at the end of the hall. It was

bright and cheery, with copper pots hanging from nails, and stained glass in the windows. Coach Rocklin stood by the table with a cellular phone pressed to her ear.

She was looking the other way and didn't see Harley come in. Harley started to say something, but Coach Rocklin spoke first.

"I told you," she snarled into the phone. "I already have the girl. The boy is still at the car. I've confirmed his identity."

A chill shivered through Harley that had nothing to do with the temperature. She stepped back into the hallway and listened.

"Yes," the track coach said into the phone. "Yes. Look, with what I gave her, she won't be a problem for hours. Concentrate on the boy, got it? We need to hurry if we're going to get to him before Legion shows up."

Harley looked down at the empty coffee cup in her hand. Whatever had been in there, she was willing to bet it was a lot stronger than coffee. She was suddenly very aware that she had left her gun back at the car. Harley had to get out. She had to get to Noah before someone else did. She turned and tiptoed back down the hallway and across the living room. There was a clatter behind her and the sound of approaching steps. Harley shoved the front door open and ran outside.

Chickens squawked and flapped out of her way as she dashed across the yard. As she reached the gravel road, she heard the door swinging open at her back. "Wait!" shouted Coach Rocklin. "Where are you going?"

Harley turned off the road and plunged into the bare trees of the orchard. Branches tore at her clothing and scratched her face, but she kept running.

Gravel crunched behind her. Coach Rocklin was following.

"There's nowhere to go, Harley!" shouted the coach. "Come back before you hurt yourself!"

Harley made another turn, cut across two lines of trees, then turned and ran along the row again. It was beginning to get dark, and it was gloomy among the tightly spaced trees. Harley thought for a moment about stopping and trying to hide. She was tired, and her legs hurt. But fear, both for herself and for Noah, drove her to keep running.

"We're trying to help you, Harley!" shouted Coach Rocklin. "You don't know what you're doing!"

Mud stuck to the soles of Harley's shoes. With each step her feet seemed to become heavier. The ache in her legs grew more sharp. A branch caught in her hair, pulling so hard that it almost jerked Harley off her feet. She lowered her head and ran on.

There was a crackle of breaking branches behind her. Harley risked turning her head for a moment and saw the small form of Coach Rocklin running down the next row. Running was the wrong word. Coach Rocklin was *flying*, ripping through the orchard at a pace that would have set a world-record mile. She was close, and she was catching up fast.

"Come on!" shouted the coach. "It's for your own good!" She didn't even sound winded.

Harley wanted to shout back a reply, but she had no breath for it. Instead she turned left and charged across the rows again, suffering slaps and slashes from branches in her way. Headlights flickered through the trees ahead of her and she heard the sound of a passing car. The highway was close. Her breath coming in painful gasps, Harley sprinted for the road.

Hands closed on her shoulders. With incredible, impossible strength, she was lifted clean off her feet and hurled through the branches. The world spun around Harley as she sailed into the trees, and then down to strike the ground with stunning force.

"Idiot," snarled Coach Rocklin.

Stars danced across Harley's vision as she rolled over and looked at the woman. "You're not trying to help me," Harley said. There was a bright taste of blood in her mouth.

Coach Rocklin walked toward her. Her arms were held at her sides, her fingers curled like claws. Her face was twisted with rage. "You have no idea what I'm trying to do," she said. "I was put in this position just so I could keep an eye over you. We've thought of everything."

Harley felt the ground at her side. Her fingers closed on a heavy broken branch, as thick as a baseball bat and as long as Harley's arm. She climbed to her feet, holding the branch in both hands.

"Stay back," said Harley. She swung the branch through the air.

Coach Rocklin laughed. "Put that down and come with me. It's for the best."

Harley backed away, still swinging the branch. "You're with Unit 17, aren't you."

"This is all for the best, Harley. We're here to help."

"People who are trying to help me don't try to drug me," Harley retorted.

"It's better than what Legion will do if they get to you first." The small woman stopped. Her face slowly relaxed and she held her hands up palms out. "Look, I won't try to hurt you," she said in a calm, reasonable voice. "Let's just talk this out, okay? You don't want to fight me."

The weight of the branch seemed to grow in Harley's hands. She let the tip drop to the ground. "All right," she said wearily. "What's Legion?"

Coach Rocklin sprang forward like a cheetah. Harley raised the branch and tried to strike, but the coach caught the blow easily, twisting the branch free. She looked into Harley's face. "*Fool*," she hissed.

Harley kicked her in the knee.

It was a blow that should have crippled her, but Coach Rocklin only dropped the branch and hopped back. An angry growl came from her lips.

Harley snatched up the branch and swung again. This time her blow struck home, smashing into the coach's ribs.

Rocklin staggered and bent over at the waist.

Harley stepped back, took a better grip on the branch, and swung with all her strength.

The swing connected against Coach Rocklin's head with enough force to hit a home run out of any ballpark. The branch cracked. Rocklin dropped to her knees as Harley staggered back.

When Coach Rocklin looked up, there was a wide gash in her forehead. Fluid ran down her face and dripped from her chin in a syrupy stream. It was dark in the orchard, almost night, but it was not too dark for Harley to see that what was oozing from the coach's face was not blood. It was thick and sticky, and as clear as water.

Harley stared at her in shock. "What . . . what *are* you?"

The coach's eyes blazed. "More than you will ever know," she said in a low grating voice. Then Rocklin's eyes blinked closed, and her head slumped over to the side. She was out cold.

Harley turned and ran.

Noah opened his eyes and found himself in another strange dream. In this one, he was trapped in some odd, small space, held down by painfully tight straps. The sky had turned muddy brown.

It took him a good ten seconds to realize that he was still in Harley's car. Only the car was upside down.

Noah swung in his shoulder harness. His head pounded with every beat of his heart, and his stomach seemed on the point of exploding. He fumbled for the release on his seat belt, pressed it, and fell in a heap against the roof of the car.

"Harley?"

The driver's seat was empty. The straps of Harley's seat belt dangled down.

"Harley!" Noah shouted. "Harley, are you out there?" There was no reply.

Something glittered on the floor—formerly the roof—of the car. Noah dug among the trash that had collected there and came out with the dark pistol Harley had been carrying. He was glad enough to have the gun, but seeing it only made him worry more about Harley. He had to get out and find her.

The window on Noah's side was half buried in mud, rock, and shrubs. He had to lie on his back and press his feet against his car seat to push himself through the small opening. He squeezed out the slot and fell into the weeds at the side of the wreck, completely covered in mud.

Noah got to his feet and stood ankle deep in the swampy water. He was dizzy, and he felt as if someone had beaten him with a baseball bat from head to toe.

"Harley?" he called.

The wind coming through the trees was the only answer. Harley was gone. A lump wedged in Noah's throat. The people that had run them off the road had obviously been trying to kill them. If those people now had Harley . . .

Noah forced the thought from his head. He would find Harley—that was all there was to it. From the color of the sky, it was getting late. He could climb up the hill, or he could walk along the valley until he reached his car. "Heads or tails," he said to himself.

He picked tails. If Harley had been taken by someone, Noah was not likely to catch them on foot. If she was walking on her own, he might even catch up to her. He sloshed through the swampy ground around the wreck and started walking toward his car.

It was not easy walking. The woods here were not the neat, clear trees found around the base. There were trees of all sizes tangled together with vines, shrubs, rotted logs, and cockleburs. Where the woods opened up there were mud puddles, piles of rock, or small patches of marsh. All of it seemed designed to get tangled around Noah's feet and slow his progress. As the light leaked out of the sky, shadows gathered in the hollow, making the footing even more treacherous.

When the light first appeared among the trees ahead, Noah thought it was the street light from the parking lot. He increased his pace, hurrying toward it. But street lights weren't red. And street lights didn't move.

Noah stopped his march through the tangled woods. The light grew brighter. Closer. Noah began to step slowly backward, his face still turned to the woods ahead. He fumbled with Harley's gun, trying to cock it without looking.

It was quiet. A moment earlier night birds had been calling. Now they were silent, hiding. The shadows shifted around Noah as the light grew closer. A red glow gleamed from the damp ground. Pools of water turned to blood in the gory light. The glow grew brighter, then dimmer, then brighter again as the source moved among the trees. Shafts of red light slipped between the trunks.

Noah trembled. He had been waiting for something like this. Looking for it. But now that it was here, he found that he was consumed with fear.

Slowly, pulsing like a beating heart, the sphere emerged from the woods.

It was smaller than any UFO Noah had ever read about, no more than five or six feet across. It didn't zip across the sky. There was no row of lighted windows. The whole thing *was* light—a sphere of brilliant illumination the color of fresh blood. It made a faint crackling hiss as it floated through the wood, the sound of a radio tuned to an empty channel.

Noah's mouth fell open. A feeling came over him that was so strong he felt it in his bones. It was more than fear, more than excitement. As the sphere grew closer, Noah let out a thin cry. He didn't know whether to cheer or to scream.

The light paused over a patch of mire. It pulsed larger, growing to ten feet in diameter. A beam of red light shot down and swept across the surface of the marsh. Where it touched, brown grass crackled and the moist ground steamed. The beam winked out. The sphere dropped down to a smaller size and began moving forward again.

Noah could feel its approach on his skin. It wasn't heat so much as an *itch*—as though a thousand ants had been turned loose all over his body.

The sphere drew closer, its hissing sound growing into a roar. It approached until it was no more than twenty feet away, its crimson light covering him. Then it stopped. It pulsed faster, throbbing in and out, in and out, with a pace that quickly became a blur. With the pulsing came a warbling, whistling hum. Then, in a split second, the sphere shrank down to the size of a basketball.

As it grew smaller, its light grew more intense. Noah gasped and threw his hands over his eyes as the fiery light reached a blinding brightness. Now there was heat. It felt like the door of a blast furnace had opened to breathe fire down on Noah. The hum rose into a shriek.

Gray mist gathered around Noah, and with it came the circling faces. He smelled that sharp scent that reminded him of hospitals.

"Not now!" he begged. "I have to see this!"

His feet slipped on the damp ground as he struggled against the dream. He fell into mud that was so hot, it bubbled in his ears. Around him pale phantoms, tattered pieces of the dream, shifted against a background of fire.

"Insertion was nominal," said a voice, but this time it was faint, no more than a whisper. "Attempting . . . link . . . functional." The voice faded, and with it went both the ghosts of the circling faces and the burning red light.

The sphere was gone.

Noah sat up and peered into the trees, trying to catch a glimpse of the red glow. All around him, a mist rose from the seared ground. A sour, burned-meat smell hung in the air.

Noah's clothing was charred at the edges. The pistol in his right hand was so hot he was surprised the bullets didn't explode. He put his left hand to his hair and found it matted into charred curls at the ends. Moving his hand down, he discovered that his eyebrows were scorched, too. His face felt like he had spent a week on the beach without sunscreen.

A tremor ran through Noah's body and an unexpected burst of laughter escaped his lips. Another followed. For long minutes, he rocked back and forth on the steaming earth, shaking with howls of uncontrollable laughter. It was real. They were real. If this sphere existed, then anything was possible. Every detail from his dreams, no matter how crazy, could be real. And if Noah wasn't nuts, it meant that someone really was out to kill him. Somehow, even knowing that was better than worrying about losing his mind.

When the laughing fit had passed, Noah suddenly

remembered Harley. He felt a stab of guilt and climbed to his feet. He hurried on.

After another five minutes of walking, he stumbled out on the parking lot at Lake Malone State Park. A single street light burned at the end of the lot, shining down on Noah's blue Mustang. He felt a burst of relief so great it almost started him laughing again.

Noah ran to the car. He fumbled his keys out of his pocket, climbed inside, and shoved the pistol under his seat. Ten seconds later he was roaring out of the parking lot.

His mind raced as he sped down the highway. If Harley had been captured, she might have been taken back to the base. He would have to go after her—if he could figure out a way to get in without Harley's help. Maybe Mr. Janes could do something.

He was concentrating so intently on getting back to town that he didn't notice the ragged, muddy figure in the road until he was almost on her.

Noah yelled in surprise, smashing the brakes against the floorboard. The Mustang skidded, slewed around, and screeched to a halt.

The thin, mud-streaked figure staggered over to the car. "Noah?" Harley asked. "Is that you?"

Noah stared at her in amazement. "You look . . ." He paused. Even as tired as he was, he realized that there was no way to finish that sentence without getting in trouble. "Are you all right?"

"I'm not sure," Harley replied. She ran around the car and jumped in on the other side. "Let's get out of here. Quick."

Noah had no problem with that. He got the Mustang's nose pointed in the right direction and headed for town.

He glanced over at Harley. "I can't believe you're really here. I was afraid I would never see you again."

"I was worried about the same thing," Harley told him quietly.

"How did you get out of the car?"

"I climbed out," she said. She pulled down the visor and frowned at the reflection in the mirror. "Some pretty strange things have happened since then."

"Did you see it, too?" Noah asked.

"See what?"

"The sphere. The ball of light."

The expression Harley gave him was answer enough. "No," she said. "I didn't see that." She shook her head. "I think I'd be less surprised if I did."

Noah listened as Harley explained her encounter with Coach Rocklin. "What do you mean it wasn't blood?" he asked.

Harley looked down, her muddy hair falling over her face. "I'm not sure anymore," she admitted. "I was hurt. Maybe I was seeing things."

"And maybe you weren't," Noah replied. He took his right hand off the wheel and took hold of Harley's left. Both their hands were dirty, but the grip was warm and comforting.

When they pulled up to Dee's house, both Dee and her father were waiting outside. As soon as Noah was out of the car, Dee had her arms around him.

"They found the car out by the highway," she

said. "We thought you'd been crunched." She kissed Noah on the cheek, then ran over to hug Harley. "You guys can't stay out of trouble for ten minutes."

"I think a trip to the hospital is in order," said Mr. Janes. "You two need to see a doctor."

"No," Noah and Harley said together.

"We're all right," added Noah. "We're just dirty."

Dee's father had a grim expression on his face. "From the looks of that car, you didn't roll down that hill by accident."

"Someone forced us off the road," Harley told him.

Dee's father grimaced. "Do you know who did it?" he asked.

"It was a big car," Noah recalled. "Black. I didn't get a look at anyone inside."

Dee's father glanced at the cars passing on the road. "Let's get in the house. We've got more to talk about." Once inside, he produced two more print-outs. "Here's the word on your Ian Cain," he said. "Looks like quite a hero. Two citations. Participated in some very important cases."

Harley glanced at the sheet, then handed it across to Noah. The picture on the page had the grainy look of a fax, but it was clear enough to make out Cain's lantern jaw and deep-set eyes. "So Cain's for real," Noah said.

"Oh, yeah," Dee's father agreed. "Only Ian Cain retired better than ten years ago."

Noah blinked at Mr. Janes. "What?"

The policeman pointed to the paper. "According to this birth date, your man would be about sixty years old by now."

"That can't be right," Harley said. "The guy we talked to was no more than thirty, tops."

"If he was," said Dee's father, "then he wasn't Ian Cain. But this other sheet is the one that's bothering me the most." He shuffled the papers in his hands. "What I have here is a bulletin telling me to be on the lookout for one Kara Martinez."

"Who's that?" asked Noah.

Dee's father held up the sheet. "Look familiar?" Coming through the fax machine had made the image coarse, but the subject was unmistakable.

Harley grabbed the paper out of his hand. "It's me," she said.

"Yep." The policeman folded his arms across his chest. "If you hadn't come to me before this came out, and if I hadn't seen what happened to your father's records, I'd probably be locking you up right now. Notice that they say they want you for questioning and don't list you as dangerous. Whoever's behind this, they want you taken alive."

Noah took the paper from Harley's hand and stared at the black-and-white image. It was unmistakably her picture, but it seemed subtly more menacing. The expression was sullen, the eyes shadowed. Below the picture was a list of offenses that included fraud, selling drugs, and robbery.

Harley rocked back in her chair. Noah saw that under the streaks of dirt, her pretty face was pale and tight. "What about my real records?" she asked.

"Gone," said Dee's father. "As far as everyone else is concerned, Kathleen Davisidaro never existed."

FIFTEEN

Harley pulled a brier-studded vine away from her leg. "Ouch," she complained. "Maybe we should have gone for the trunk."

"You wouldn't say that if you'd tried it," said Noah's voice out of the darkness.

With the tall fence of Tulley Hill Base on their right, the two pushed on through clumps of shrubs and small trees. At least this time they didn't have far to walk. After only a hundred yards, bright light shown through the trees. Harley slowed, doing her best to move quietly. "I can see the gate," she said. "We're almost there." She edged forward until she was about a dozen yards from the gate.

Noah came up beside her in the darkness. "We shouldn't have long to wait," he whispered.

The words were barely out of his mouth when the distant whine of a police siren cut through the night air. Seconds later, a black-and-white patrol car pulled up at the gate with its lights flashing. The siren cut off, and Mr. Janes climbed out of the car. "Open the gate!" he shouted.

A guard emerged from the blockhouse. "What do you want?"

"I have information that a missing child may be on your property," said Mr. Janes. "I'm here to investigate."

"You have no jurisdiction here," said the guard.

Harley edged forward along the fence. The lights from the police car swung over her, casting shadows of red and blue. She crouched low and inched toward the gate.

"I can't allow you into the base without clearance," said the guard.

"Well, I'm not going anywhere until you do," replied Dee's father. "In fact, I think I'll call in a few of the state boys. You think your commander would listen to ten troopers better than he will to me?"

"Hang on," said the guard. His voice was little more than a growl. "I'll bring someone down here to talk."

Harley froze and watched as the guard marched back to the booth. She couldn't make out what he was saying into the microphone there, but she could make out the angry tone. After a few seconds, he came marching back.

"One of the commander's assistants will be here shortly," he said.

"Well, he better be ready to let me in," said Dee's father. He thumped his finger against the chest of the guard. "This is official business and—" The policeman broke off in the middle of his talk. "What's that over there?" he asked, pointing off to the left.

The guard turned around. "Where?"

As soon as he turned, Harley tiptoed behind his back to the guard booth. She slipped silently through the door, slid to the hard floor, and lay still.

"There," said Mr. Janes. "See that light?"

Harley knew that somewhere out in the night, Dee was pointing her flashlight toward the gate. She hoped

Dee was far enough away to avoid getting caught.

"I don't see anything," said the voice of the guard.

"Over there!" shouted Dee's father. "Are you blind?"

Harley heard the hard thump of the guard's boots on the blacktop outside. "All right," he barked. "I *do* see a light, but it's well outside the boundaries of the base."

While he was speaking, Noah eased himself through the door of the guard booth and crouched next to Harley.

"There's a vehicle coming toward the gate," Noah whispered. "I saw headlights."

Harley nodded. A moment later, she heard the whine of electric motors as the gate opened.

"Wait," Noah said, his hand on Harley's arm. "Wait."

Lights swung past the guard booth as the vehicle left the base. There was a click, and the tone of the motors changed as the gate began to close.

Harley peeked around the edge of the door. She could see Mr. Janes waving his arms heatedly at the guard, whose broad, tense back was still turned to the booth.

"We're clear," she whispered.

"*Now,*" Noah hissed. He jumped from the booth.

Harley got to her feet and sprang after him. Noah slipped through the closing gate with two feet to spare. Harley made it by an inch.

They kept running as silently as humanly possible up the road inside the base, sprinting for the trees. Harley hoped with each stride that the darkness and

Mr. Janes's distractions were enough to prevent the guard from noticing their run. She stumbled to a stop only when Noah grabbed her arm and pulled her up short. They had made it safely to the cover of the dark woods.

"I think . . . I think he didn't see us," she panted.

Noah nodded. He leaned over, hands on knees as he caught his breath. "I don't hear any sirens or anything."

"So, where do we go from here?" asked Harley.

"Would you like my suggestion?" said a new voice.

Harley's heart leapt into her throat. She turned and saw a red glow. Her first thought was the glowing sphere that Noah had described, but after a moment she saw that it was a flashlight covered in red plastic. In the soft red light stood Ian Cain.

"Are you . . . ," started Harley in a loud voice. Then she remembered where she was and lowered the volume. "Are you trying to scare us to death?"

"I'm sorry," Cain said with a smile. "There's little opportunity to make a nice introduction when—"

"And *hey*," Harley interrupted, narrowing her eyes at Cain. "Give me back my father's journals."

". . . when you're sneaking around in a top-secret base," Cain finished calmly.

"I know you took them," Harley told him.

Cain sighed. "Yes, I removed the journals from your possession," he admitted. "For your own protection. There are dangerous groups who would like to get their hands on those notebooks. I will return them when I deem the time to be right. For right now, the further away you are from them, the safer you will be."

"Somebody's *already* trying to have us killed," Harley pointed out.

"Which groups?" Noah asked. "Legion? Unit 17?"

Cain nodded. "Among others. Again, the less you know, the safer you will be. Believe it or not, but you are lucky it was I who found you first."

"*How* did you find us?" Harley asked.

"I don't find *you*," said Cain. "I find *him*." He raised the flashlight and shone the red beam on Noah.

Noah shielded his eyes from the light. "How?"

Cain's light shifted away as he dug into the pocket of his coat. "With this," he said. He produced a thin gray rod that had a dull metallic gleam under the red light. Cain pointed the rod toward Noah. Immediately a line of small green lights glowed along the side of the rod. It began to emit a high-pitched whine. Cain pointed the rod away. The lights flickered and went off. The whine stopped.

"There's a device implanted below the skin at the base of your right shoulder blade," Cain told Noah cheerfully.

"There's *what?*" Noah shouted. His outraged voice was loud enough to make Harley wince. His hand flew to his shoulder. "There's something *inside* me?"

A sudden memory struck her. "Insertion is nominal," Harley said. "Telemetry is . . ." She shook her head. "I don't remember the rest."

Noah looked at her strangely. "Where did you hear that?"

"From you," Harley replied. "It's part of what you

said when you were having one of your dreams."

"Most likely it's what was said during the implantation of the device," said Cain. "They use a hypnogogic paralysis technique. Stress often induces flashback."

Noah rubbed his hand along his right side. "That's what I've been remembering," he said softly. "That's where the dreams come from." He looked at Cain. "Who are they? Why did they do this to me?"

Cain smiled. His teeth were red in the glow from the light. "They call themselves Legion," he said. "Though there are not as many of them as the name might suggest."

"Legion?" Harley asked. "Coach Rocklin said something about Legion. Who are they?"

"It's difficult to explain," Cain replied. "Let's just say that Legion doesn't get along well with Unit 17. And the feeling is mutual."

"It was Legion who put this thing in my back?" Noah shook his head. "Why?"

"They used it to keep track of you," Cain answered. "But I changed the frequency so they can't anymore."

"But *why* are they tracking me?" Noah asked again. "What do I have to do with anything?"

Cain chuckled. "I'm as curious about that as you are," he said. "If you find out, please let me know."

"But what about the aliens?"

Cain stood silent for a moment. "There are no aliens," he said at last.

Noah stepped closer to the agent, his hands tensed into fists at his sides. "You're lying. I've seen them. I've seen the flying spheres."

Cain raised his hands in a calming gesture. "Not everything is as it seems, Mr. Templer. I've said too much already."

"Can you tell me why Unit 17 took my father?" Harley asked.

Cain's expression was grim. "I'm afraid your father is deeply involved in this affair, Ms. Davisidaro. His work is not what you have been lead to believe."

Harley thought of the strange entries in her father's notebooks. "What do you mean?" she asked. "What's in those notebooks?"

"That's for another time," replied Cain.

Noah shook his head. "No," he said. "You tell her what's going on with her father. And you tell me what's going on with my dreams. You tell us right now." Noah's voice had a cold, hard edge that Harley had never heard before. He reached into his pocket and came out with something black and shiny. It took Harley a moment to realize it was the pistol.

"And just what do you intend to do with that?" asked Cain haughtily. He didn't seem the least upset by the appearance of the gun.

Noah raised the gun until the short barrel was pointed at Cain's face. "Tell me what's behind my dreams."

"Or you'll kill me?" Cain asked. He shook his head. "I hardly think—"

There was a click as Noah thumbed back the hammer on the revolver. "Tell me," he said. "Now."

Cain raised his hands. "I can't," he said.

Harley stepped up to Noah's side. "Noah, don't do this." At that moment, she was more frightened of Noah than she was of Cain.

Noah continued to stare at the tall agent. Slowly, he lowered the gun until it was directed at Cain's legs. "I won't kill you," Noah said.

"I'm glad to hear it," said Cain.

"But I will shoot your knee off," Noah added. He put his face close to the revolver and sighted down the short barrel. "I understand it hurts a lot."

Cain sighed. "You have no idea," he said. "But whatever you might do to me, it's nothing next to what will happen to me should I divulge the information you seek."

Noah's arm trembled. For a second, Harley was sure he was going to shoot. Then Noah's arm dropped to his side. He turned and looked off into the darkness. "I should have shot you," he said in a choked voice.

Cain lowered his hands. "I'm glad you chose otherwise," he said. The agent's voice was still irritatingly calm. "Believe me, withholding this information is in your own best interest."

His words reminded Harley of her encounter with Coach Rocklin. "Are you with Legion?" she asked.

The agent shook his head. "No."

"Then who?"

Cain's deep eyes glittered in the red light. "My employers are another matter I cannot discuss."

Noah turned back toward Harley. "Come on," he said. "If this jerk isn't going to give us any answers, we'll have to go get our own." He walked off through the woods.

Harley started to follow, but Cain waved his red light. "Not tonight," he called.

Noah stopped and looked over his shoulder. "What?"

"There's been a change in plans," said Cain. "You can't enter the base tonight."

"Why not?" asked Harley. "You were the one that wanted us to go in there again."

The agent clicked his flashlight off, plunging them all into darkness. "Plans have changed," he said. "You'll have to wait."

"Wait for what?" Harley said angrily. "They've taken my father, and now they've got me branded a criminal. You want me to wait until I show up on *America's Most Wanted?*"

For a moment there was nothing but the sound of wind whistling through the leafless trees. Harley squinted into the darkness, wondering if the agent was still there.

Then Cain's voice drifted out of the night. "If you go into the base tonight," he said. "You will almost certainly die."

"Why?" asked Noah. "What makes tonight so special?"

Again Cain was slow to answer. "Others are expected here tonight. And when they arrive, this will become a very unhealthy place to be."

Harley took a step toward the source of that voice. "Someone's going to attack the base? What will happen to my father?"

"And Caroline?" added Noah.

There was no reply.

Harley clenched her hands into fists. "We're going in there," she said. "You stay out here and be nice and safe." Noah nodded, and immediately started walking in the direction of the strange buildings. Harley followed.

They had gone several yards when Cain called after them. "There's a car in front of your house!" he shouted. "Take it. You've got no more than twenty minutes."

"Twenty minutes?" Harley squinted into the darkness. "How do we get out?"

This time the silence stretched on and on.

"I think he's gone," Noah said at last. "And we better get going, too. The clock's ticking."

A green car was waiting in the driveway where Cain had said it would be. On the front seat were two pairs of blue coveralls and caps like those worn by the base personnel.

"Cain must have just learned that these people are coming," said Noah. "It looks like he had things prepared for us to go in."

"Or maybe he never expected us to listen to him," Harley suggested.

It took them a couple of their precious minutes to slide into the coveralls. The night was cold, but as Harley climbed into the car she noticed she was sweating. "Are you ready?" she asked.

Noah shook his head. "No, but let's go anyway."

Harley started the car with trembling fingers and pulled out onto the road.

They drove past the office buildings, around the control tower, and down the alley between the slab-sided hangers. Finally, the car's headlights illuminated the wire mesh of the inner gate.

Harley pulled up as close as she could to the glowing security card box and pulled out the pass card Cain had given her. "Cross your fingers," she said. Then she dipped the card into the slot.

The delay was just long enough to make Harley's heart miss a beat. Then the green light flashed on. This time there was no alarm. No bright lights. Instead the inner gate rolled slowly to the side. They were in.

"Now what?" Harley asked as she drove through the gate. There were other cars parked alongside the complex, but she saw no sign of a door.

"Over there," said Noah. He pointed to what looked like a big pipe jutting into the parking area. "The cars are grouped around that thing. I'll bet there's an entrance."

Harley pulled over. She thumped the gearshift into park and stared at the massive building. She picked up the cap from the car seat and pulled it down on her head.

"All right," she said. "Let's go find my dad."

They stepped out of the car and walked to the mouth of the pipe. At first glance there was no opening, only a wall of flat featureless metal. Harley ran her hands over the smooth surface. "Are you sure this is the way in?"

"Here," Noah pointed out. "Look."

There was a thin slot in the center of the pipe, a slot just big enough to accept the security card. Harley inserted the black card. At once there was a wet, slurping sound, like a thick milk shake being pulled through a thin straw. A small hole appeared in the center of the wall. It widened rapidly, opening like a camera iris, until it was a circle six feet across.

Through the opening, Harley saw a hallway with rounded walls and a flat floor, composed of something dark blue, glossy, and organic-looking. A thin line of pale green light gleamed from the ceiling. The whole thing looked like it had been *grown* instead of built—like a coral reef, or the inside of a hornets' nest.

She shivered. "I don't think we're in Kansas anymore."

"Yeah," Noah agreed. "I'm not sure we're on this planet." He stepped past Harley into the mouth of the pipe. "Come on. We've only got about ten minutes left."

The blue pipe led them to another hallway, this one colored a queasy mustard yellow. So far they had not seen another living person.

"Which way?" Harley asked.

Noah shook his head. "Shh," he said. "Listen."

Harley tipped her head to the side. After a moment, she heard a distant crackle, followed by a throbbing hum. "It sounds like paper being crumpled."

"It sounds like the thing I saw in the woods," said Noah. "Let's go."

He walked quickly down the hallway to their left. Another intersection came up. A red tube, made of the same strange, organic-looking material as the blue and yellow tubes—almost like the stuff butterflies use to make their chrysalis. This time the sound led to the right. A few feet in, the pipe turned upward, rising in a gradually steepening curve.

"Where is everyone?" Harley asked as they trudged up the long slope. "With all those cars outside, I expected this place to be crowded."

Noah shrugged. "It's a big place. Someone's got to be here."

The red pipe ended at a wall of flat, shiny metal. The popping, snapping, hissing sound was much louder now. Joining it was a growling hum so low and intense that Harley didn't really hear it—she felt it reverberating in her bones.

"It's here," said Noah. There was excitement in his voice. He laid his hand against the wall. "It's right here."

Harley stepped past him. "Let's hope my dad's here, too."

She slid the pass card into the slot at the side of the wall. Again there was that disturbingly wet noise, and an opening grew in the center of the wall.

The space beyond was so vast that Harley swayed with dizziness. A bone white platform extended an arm's reach from the door. Beyond that there was nothing but air.

Harley eased forward carefully. With each step, more of the room below her was revealed.

"It's like being inside a computer," said Noah. He looked around a moment longer. "A really big computer."

"A crazy computer," Harley added. Around them ran cables of all sizes and colors. Hair-thin fibers sprung from the walls to join and form wires that twisted together into cables thicker than Harley's legs. Faint lights blinked high in the tangled mass along the roof. Traces of shining copper ran down the walls in cascades of frozen metal. Posts of ceramic and glass reared toward the roof like glistening redwoods. Everything in the room looked like it had been heated to melting, and then had been cooled, leaving no crisp edges or square angles.

Noah stepped out onto the white platform. His blue eyes were fixed on the floor below. He opened his mouth and gave a wordless moan.

"What is it?" Harley asked.

Noah pointed to the far side of the room. "Over there," he said.

Fighting against the feeling that she was going to fall, Harley stood beside him and looked down.

Over a hundred feet below and across the vast room, almost hidden by the cables and pillars which filled the room, was a glowing sphere of light. It was white, blazing, almost blindingly bright, and a good twenty feet in diameter. Spots of color rose up on the sphere, and then faded. Blue arcs of static electricity snaked out from the base and danced along the gleaming metal floor.

Something was moving inside the sphere. At first Harley could only see a vague smudge within the brightness. Slowly, from the chaos of boiling light, a dark shape took form.

Harley shielded her eyes, trying to see through the glare. The form focused, becoming more distinct. She saw arms and legs, a face, dark hair, and olive skin. Finally, the form pulled free from the light and stood on the platform. It was a man.

Harley felt a tingle which had nothing to do with the sphere. The man was too far away to make out his features, but there was something in his form, something in the way he moved, that was painfully familiar.

"That's my dad," she whispered.

A sinking sensation struck Noah. He staggered and turned around to find himself facing a solid wall. His palms slid over the shiny metal as the wall slid past. The platform was descending.

"Dad!" Harley shouted.

Noah turned and saw Harley standing at the edge of the platform, waving her arms in the air. Noah grabbed her and pulled her back.

"Careful," he warned. "It's a long way down."

Harley tugged free of his arms. "That's my *father*," she told him roughly.

Noah peered through the cables at the glowing sphere. He saw what looked like a man standing beside the light, but against the brilliant glare he couldn't see any more than that. "Are you sure it's him?"

"Yeah." Harley nodded. "I'm sure."

Noah glanced at his watch. If Cain was right, they had less than five minutes. "Hang on," he said. "We're going in the right direction."

The platform slowly dropped between tangled masses of cables that seemed to have no design or purpose. As they went down, the temperature rose. Sweat rolled down Noah's face and dripped from his chin. The twisting stands of colored cables grew ever thicker, forming sheets, webs, and bundles as thick as trees. Further down, huge rods of something slick and shiny jutted up to meet the mass of cables. Noah

183

felt like he was being lowered into a jungle rain forest of metal and glass.

The platform reached the bottom with a soft thump. Noah and Harley stepped off.

"Come *on*," Harley urged. "Let's go get him."

"Wait," Noah snagged the back of her coveralls and pulled her back. "Look over there," he whispered in her ear.

Standing in the shadows of this strange high-tech jungle were hundreds of people.

Some of them stood alone, and others were clustered in small groups. All of them wore blue coveralls identical to the ones Cain had given Noah and Harley. And all of them had the same blank glassy-eyed expressions on their faces.

The hairs on the back of Noah's neck bristled. The people stared at the sphere of light without moving or speaking, without even blinking.

"They've been hypnotized," Harley said.

Noah nodded. "Maybe that'll help," he said hopefully. "Maybe they won't see us."

"There's only one way to find out," Harley decided. She set off across the room, walking slowly, but steadily, among the forest of wires.

Noah followed behind. He tensed as they approached the first group of people, but the men and women they passed didn't even turn their heads as Noah strode past.

They were still a hundred feet away from the sphere when shadows flickered over the vast room. A new form was beginning to stir within the light. Another man emerged from the glow, and then a woman with hair as red as polished copper. The light was still too bright for Noah to make out any features of the people's faces. The two newcomers lined up beside the sphere, standing next to the man Harley said was her father.

Noah hurried to catch up to Harley. "You know who those other people are?" he asked.

"No," Harley replied. There was a puzzled look on her face. "I can't understand what my father's doing. Why doesn't he get away from them?" She bit her lip. "Maybe it's not him."

"He might be under their control," said Noah. "Like all the people in this room. I mean, just look at—" He broke off in midsentence.

Standing alone next to a pillar of blue glass was a small figure. Even with her thick brown hair tucked up into a blue cap, Noah had no trouble recognizing the heart-shaped face.

"Caroline?" Noah hurried over to her. "Can you hear me, Caroline?" The young woman's face was fixed on the glowing sphere. White sparks reflected in her green eyes. Her skin looked pale as chalk under the brilliant white glow. "Caroline, wake up. It's Noah."

Caroline blinked. It was a terribly slow movement, her lids moving down and up as if it cost her a tremendous effort. With her eyes half closed, Caroline turned toward Noah.

Noah felt a rush of relief. "Caroline," he said. "We've come to take you home."

Her lips opened slightly. Then she screamed.

It was a high, inhuman sound, delivered with

such force that Noah staggered back. Surprise stole his breath away, as the scream raised goose bumps on his skin.

Caroline stepped toward him, her hand lifted to point at Noah and Harley. "Invaders!" she shrieked. "Interlopers!"

A cold wind passed through the thick tropical air. All around the room, faces turned away from the sphere and toward the two visitors. Figures in blue began to stir, moving toward Harley and Noah like the walking dead from an old horror movie.

Noah spun away from Caroline. His heart raced as he looked left and right. From every hidden recess of the room, more figures appeared. They didn't rush. They walked toward Noah and Harley with a slow, steady pace that was more frightening than any run.

Harley backed up beside Noah, her arm pressed against his. "What now?" she asked. Already dozens of blue figures were closing in on them, and dozens more were appearing every moment.

A dark opening along one wall caught Noah's eye. "Over there," he said softly, pointing with a tip of his chin. "It might be a way out."

Harley's forehead creased with distress. "But my father—"

"We can't do anything now," Noah interrupted. "We have to get ourselves out of here. We have to be *alive* to help him." He took one step toward the wall he'd indicated before unbelievably powerful fingers clamped down on his arm.

Noah was shoved down on the smooth, glossy floor. A boot smashed into his ribs. Gasping for breath, he braced himself for the next blow. When it didn't come, he slowly raised his head and looked around.

Harley was held tight in the grip of two tall, broad-shouldered men. One of them had his hand pressed over her mouth. Above his fingers, Harley's eyes were full of angry fire.

Standing beside her were Caroline and an older man with a neat gray mustache. Caroline stood with her arms crossed. The blank expression on her face was gone, replaced by a self-satisfied sneer.

"Hello, Noah," she said. "Don't tell me you came here to rescue me."

Noah gritted his teeth. "I didn't come here for you," he said. He put his hands on the floor and pushed himself up to his knees. "I came here for me."

The older man moved with extraordinary speed. He stepped forward, dug his fingers into Noah's floppy hair, and hauled him painfully to his feet. "Do you have any idea what you've interrupted here tonight?" barked the man.

Noah grabbed the man's arm and tried to pull loose, but it was like wrestling with a bar of steel. "Something illegal," Noah gasped. "Something the FBI would love to know about."

An amused expression crossed the man's wide face. "They would, huh? The FBI?" He shook his head and his smile faded. "Take these two out of here and kill them. They've given me enough trouble." He took his hand from Noah's hair, put it on his face, and shoved him.

The push staggered Noah, but this time he stayed

on his feet. He reached into the pocket of the cover-alls and came out with the pistol. "Stop right there," he said, holding the gun at his waist.

Caroline Crewson looked at him with undisguised fury. "You're a *dead* man," she hissed.

"Yeah?" Noah replied. "Your friend already made that threat. I've got nothing to lose." Trying to behave with a confidence he didn't feel, Noah waved the gun at the two guards holding Harley. "Now let her go." The men holding Harley didn't move. Noah thumbed back the hammer on the revolver. "You better tell them to do it," he said to Caroline.

For a moment, Caroline simply stared at Noah. Her green eyes were as cold as the winter sea. "Do it," she said at last.

The men holding Harley loosened their grip. Harley pulled loose and ran over to stand beside Noah. "That one is Colonel Braddock," she said, pointing to the man with the mustache. "He's supposed to be the base commander."

"All right," said Noah. He turned to Braddock, directing the gun at the man's stout body. "If you're in charge here, then you can tell them to let us go."

Braddock snorted. "And why should I do that?" he said. "Even if you fire every bullet in that gun, you'll be dead before you go five yards."

Noah tightened his grip on the pistol. "So will you," he said.

The commander started to reply, but before he could, a murmur of voices erupted from across the room. "They're coming through!" someone shouted.

Braddock and the others turned away. For a

moment, Noah kept his gaze fixed on Braddock. But as the man's face slipped into that blank, worshipful expression, Noah glanced to the right. What he saw froze him as surely as it did the others.

In the heart of the sphere, something was moving. White on white, a slender form began to emerge. Glowing hands came free of the light. Then a pair of impossibly thin legs. A face swam up through the light, a face with huge dark eyes.

All over the room, people broke into cheers. The noise rose to a fever pitch as the white form stepped free of the sphere.

Noah knew his mouth was hanging open, but he could do nothing about it. It was just like his dreams. The large white face with the huge black eyes. It had to be an alien.

There was more movement in the sphere, and another white form started to pull free from the light.

Noah leaned forward, trying to get a better look. And then Noah was flying.

It wasn't until he was almost on the ground that he realized that there had been an explosion. There had been no sound. The explosion itself was far too powerful to be called a sound—it was a force that carried Noah along like a leaf in an autumn wind. Glittering shards of glass and lengths of twisting cables flew with him, arcing up across the room, and then down in a heap of debris. He landed painfully on his shoulder, showered with bits and chunks of shrapnel that pocked his skin. When the explosion had passed, Noah's stunned ears heard only a faint ringing.

Shadows grew at the edge of Noah's vision that had nothing to do with his dreams. Dizzy and sick to his stomach, he sat up. Sharp pains came from his head, his shoulders, and his legs. The sleeve over his left arm had been shredded and blood seeped from a series of thin slashes in his skin. But he could see others around him who had suffered far worse.

A body lay on the floor near his feet. Noah couldn't tell if it was a man or a woman, but he could tell it was definitely dead. Other figures ran or stumbled through the room, moving through clouds of smoke and stepping over fallen pillars.

The pistol that had been in Noah's hand was gone. He looked around, but saw no sign of the gun in all the shattered glass and metal. It didn't seem to matter. All the people in the room who could still move seemed far more concerned with getting away than with stopping Noah.

Fighting back a wave of nausea, he struggled to his feet and waved smoke away from his face. "Harley!" he shouted. Even his own voice was nothing but a faint buzz to his tortured ears.

Desperately, Noah waded through the mess. He passed a broken cable spilling a stream of brilliant blue sparks onto the floor. At another spot, thick black liquid bubbled from a wide hole in the floor.

"Harley!" Noah shouted again. He seemed to hear it a little better this time. Maybe.

Ten steps further along, he stumbled over the slim figure of a woman lying half buried in a tangle of cables. "Harley?" Noah's heart went into his throat as he knelt beside the form and carefully turned her over. The blue cap fell off, revealing long brown hair. It was Caroline. The whites of her green eyes had turned almost black with ruptured blood vessels. Her face was frozen in a scream. There was a hole in her chest big enough to hold a baseball.

Noah's stomach surged, and he pressed a hand to his mouth. He closed his eyes and lurched away from Caroline's body.

When he opened his eyes again, he saw the white glow of the sphere peeking through the veils of smoke. It was still pulsing amid all the death and destruction. Behind it was a huge gap in the building wall, an opening large enough to slide a two-story house through. Noah saw no sign of the aliens, or of the other people who had been on stage.

There was a touch on Noah's arm. He jumped and spun around to find Harley right behind him. She had a bruise across her cheek, and a thin trickle of blood dripped from her nose. She was the most beautiful sight Noah had ever seen. He wrapped his arms around her and hugged her tight.

For a moment she clung to him, but then she pushed him away. Her mouth opened and closed.

"I can't hear," said Noah. He pointed to his ears. "The explosion."

Harley frowned. She tugged at the collar of Noah's coveralls, pulling him down until she could put her face close to his ear. "My father," she shouted. "Did you see where he went?"

Noah shook his head. "No."

"He was down by the light," Harley shouted into his ear. "We should look there."

191

"We need to get out of here," said Noah. "Pretty soon somebody's going to remember to kill us."

He expected a further argument from Harley, but instead she stepped back from Noah. Her eyes went wide and she pointed over his shoulder.

A faint sound reached Noah's stunned ears, a thin *chip-chip-chip*, like a cricket warming up to chirp. He turned and saw new figures entering the room from the jagged hole in the wall. There were only five or six of them, and they were dressed in black clothing from head to toe. They held equally black rifles in their arms. When the sound came again, Noah realized it was gunfire ricocheting through the room. Chips of glass and metal stung the side of Noah's face as bullets plowed into the floor at his feet. Screams and shouts of agony penetrated his damaged hearing as the base personnel were hit by the gunshots or the shrapnel. In only a few seconds, the cavernous room had become a war zone.

Harley grabbed him by the hand and gave a sharp tug. She pointed to the opening he had seen before in the corner of the room. Then she started running, crouched over to present as small a target as possible for the random gunfire.

Noah struggled to keep up with her. The silence of the chase made everything seem incredibly vivid to his watering eyes. A heap of torn metal blocked the exit. Harley took Noah's hand, and together they climbed over the debris. On the other side, a woman lay sprawled in the aperture of the door, her body serving to keep the opening in place. They stepped over the fallen woman, went down a short hallway, and emerged in the parking area.

The chaos from the explosion wasn't confined within the walls of the building. Searchlights slid back and forth over the parking area. People milled around among the cars. Wounded sat or lay in rows along the blacktop. Guards in blue appeared with guns in their hands, but they didn't rush to get inside. Instead they kept their guns trained on the crowd.

A voice boomed from a loudspeaker. "This area has been contained. Everyone remain where you are. This area has been contained."

Noah was glad to be able to hear and understand the words. His temporary deafness was fading. "We've got to get back to the car," Noah told Harley.

Harley leaned in close. "I think we're on the wrong side of the building. This wasn't where we went in." They started for the corner of the building, still holding hands.

"Halt there!" called the loudspeaker. "Stay where you are."

"Keep walking," Noah urged.

"Stop!" called the faint voice of a guard. "Stop, or you will be shot!"

Noah quickly glanced behind him. The guard was still some distance back. The corner was close. "Run!" shouted Noah, pulling Harley's hand.

As they sprinted for the corner, Noah expected to feel the bite of a bullet at any moment. The muscles of his back were tensed, waiting for the shot that would end his life. But the shot didn't come. They cleared the corner and kept running through the aisles of vehicles in the parking lot.

They had almost reached the car when one of the

men in black stepped out from behind a minivan. "Stop there," he said in a hard, crisp voice. He leveled his rifle at Harley. "Stop where you are, or I shoot the girl."

Noah staggered to a stop. "You were . . . one of the ones . . . who attacked the base," he gasped to the black-uniformed soldier. "We're on your side."

"No," the dark figure replied. "I was always on your side, but you were never on mine." Holding the rifle with one hand, the figure reached up and peeled off his mask to reveal a thin face and a shock of pale hair.

Noah blinked. "Josh?"

Josh McQuinn glared at him with disgust etched into his hard features. "I've invested over eighteen years in you," he spat. "Eighteen years!" He pulled back the action on his black rifle. "Not to mention the ten generations that came before. You were our best, and now I fully regret that I have to kill you."

Noah shook his head in confusion. "How can you spend eighteen years on anything? *I'm* only seventeen. So are you. What do you mean, *ten generations?*"

A stunned expression came over Josh's face. "You really *don't* understand, do you?"

"Understand what?"

Josh laughed. "Everyone has been so worried about the two of you. Everyone is convinced that the girl knows Unit 17's secrets and that you know all about Legion. They're all worrying themselves to death. But you really don't know anything, do you?"

"Then let us go," Noah said.

"Maybe I will," Josh replied. He lowered his gun slightly. "Maybe it's not too late. Maybe—"

A burst of gunfire came from the corner. Noah

turned his head and saw a pair of the base guards approaching in their blue coveralls. When he turned back, Josh had fallen to the ground.

Noah dropped down beside him. "Josh!"

In obvious pain, Josh twisted his neck to look at Noah. The change in him was so extreme that Noah could do nothing but stare in shock. Josh's hair had always been pale, but now it was snow white. His cheeks had hollowed. His skin was gray.

"I placed you with your family," Josh said in a creaking voice. "I took care of—" He gasped in pain.

"Josh," Noah said softly. "No." He reached out and touched his best friend's forehead, planning to brush the pale blond hair out of Josh's eyes. But Josh's skin had slid like liquid under his fingers. Noah snatched his hand back in revulsion.

"You . . ." Josh croaked. "You don't understand your *value* to us—to *everyone*. You don't understand . . . your *potential.*"

"No, Josh," Noah replied in a tiny voice. "I don't. I don't understand any of this. Help me."

Josh uttered a wet gasp of pure suffering. "I'll . . . I'll miss you," he told Noah. "You needed me." His pale eyes closed and his head lolled to the side.

Noah grabbed Josh by the collar of his black suit. "What do you mean? Who *else* is in this? I know about you, and Caroline, and Coach Rocklin. Who *else?*"

Josh's eyes opened for a moment. They were a terrible milky white. "Everyone," he whispered.

"It can't be everyone!" shouted Noah. "Who was it that tried to kill us?"

The only answer was a rattling sigh.

Noah lowered Josh back to the ground, then stared in horror as Josh's skin turned from gray to green. Josh's lips pulled back from his yellowed teeth. His nose crumbled into a gaping hole. Pale hair fell to the blacktop in fist-size clumps. With a faint popping sound, Josh's skull collapsed inward like a rotting melon. Green fluid leaked out to sizzle on the ground.

Harley grabbed Noah by the shoulder. "Come on!" she cried. "We have to go."

Noah got to his feet and stumbled along behind Harley. He turned his head and looked back just in time to see one of the guards put his foot in a pile of empty clothes and green soup that had once been his best friend, Josh McQuinn. Noah turned around and ran faster than he ever had for any track meet. Harley was right beside him.

They made it around the next corner and Noah saw their car still waiting where they had parked it. Harley flung open the door and dived inside. The car started and Harley sent it flying across the parking lot.

The base guards stepped around the corner. As soon as they spotted the car, they began firing.

"Get down!" Harley ordered.

Noah crouched in his seat. There was a sharp crack as one of the bullets struck the car. The windshield exploded into a thousand pieces as another bullet shot through the car from back to front.

Harley swerved, but she kept driving. "We're almost at the gate!" she called.

Noah raised himself up and looked through the back window. The two guards were no more than fifty yards behind, their weapons still flaring in the darkness.

"Hang on," said Harley. She stomped on the gas and the car surged ahead.

They hit the inner gate going fifty miles an hour. The impact drove Noah's head down against the dashboard. The hood of the car buckled. Metal screamed and sparks rained down as the car ripped through the gate and continued down the road.

Noah looked over at Harley, rubbing his forehead. "Remind me to never get in your way."

Harley didn't laugh. "It was my father," she said flatly. "He was right in front of us, in the light. He was right there."

"I'm sorry," Noah told her softly. "I wish I knew what to say. My mind is reeling."

"That's okay," Harley replied. "I'm not feeling so well myself. We really did just see Josh . . . *melt*, didn't we. There's so much going on that I can barely believe. I feel like I'm trapped in a nightmare."

Noah nodded, closing his eyes. "That's what I've been saying from the beginning."

"So what do we do now?" Harley asked.

Noah popped his eyes open and stared grimly at her. "I don't know." Then he noticed that a red light was blinking on the dashboard. "What's that?" he asked.

Harley glanced down. "A sign that we're not going to get much farther in this car. Either one of those guards made a lucky shot, or we smashed the radiator getting through that gate. Either way, this crate is dead."

Bursts of steam began to leak from the warped edge of the car hood. Within a hundred yards, the engine was skipping and thumping. Their speed dropped down to thirty miles per hour, then to twenty. They rolled past the string of offices with the engine barely coughing. Ten feet beyond the commander's office, the car gave one last shudder and died.

Noah pushed open his door. "We better start running," he said. "I don't think those guards are going to forget about us this time."

"We're not going to have to run far," said Harley. She got out of the car and took off down the road. "Follow me!"

They hurried back to the houses. Harley pulled the pass card from her coveralls. "I hope this thing is still good."

"What are we going to do?" asked Noah. "Hide in here?"

"Wait and see." Harley inserted the card into the slot by the garage and the door began to go up. Inside was her gleaming black and chrome motorcycle. Harley jumped onto the bike. "Quick," she said. "Get on."

Noah climbed onto the back of the bike and put his hands around Harley's thin waist. The motorcycle started with a roar. They shot out of the garage and sped toward the gate.

Noah had never ridden on the back of a motorcycle before. Now he was hurtling along at night, faster than he had ever ridden himself, through a base filled with guards determined to shoot them. But there was something strangely comforting about riding behind Harley. She drove the bike confidently, even recklessly. Her black hair flew around Noah's face. Her body was warm against his.

As they approached the front gate, Noah saw that

it was already open. A green car moved through the opening and the gate began to close.

"Hold tight!" Harley instructed. The sound of the motorcycle rose from a roar to a full-throated scream.

"You can't crash the gate on a bike!" Noah shouted in her ear. "We need to wait for another car!" The gate was already half shut and closing fast.

Harley didn't slow. The opening in the gate was ten feet wide. Five. Two.

They flashed through the slot. Noah felt a glancing blow to his shoulder as they went past. Then they were on the highway, racing toward Stone Harbor.

Noah turned and looked behind them. Rising above the Tulley Hill Research Facility were two of the glowing spheres. A third appeared. Then a fourth.

The spheres hung over the hill, bathing the woods along the road in a brilliant white light. Then they zipped off to the north, trailing silver sparks across the sky.

For several minutes, the afterimage of their flight was burned into Noah's eyes. Then even that was gone.

Harley stared over the square of brown earth. She saw it, but she couldn't believe it. "It was right here," she said. "Our house was right here."

Noah put an arm around her shoulder and turned her back toward the police car. "Come on," he said. "Let's go see the rest."

It had been only eight hours since Noah and Harley had escaped from the Tulley Hill Research Facility. Now they were back, but the base had vanished.

The guard post outside was empty, and the gate hung open. The sign that had named the base was missing. Inside, the area was even stranger. Where the row of houses had been, there were only rectangles of bare ground and dead grass. Concrete foundations marked the place where the offices had been, but there was not so much as a piece of paper left to show their contents.

The rest of the base was no different. The control tower was gone, along with all signs of the huge hangers. All that remained was a large area of blacktop and a few spots of oil.

The inner fence was there, minus the security controls and the gate that Harley had smashed. But the biggest change of all was on the other side.

Where the strange complex had stood, with its bewildering array of pipes and towers, its tunnels and rooms, and hundreds of people, there was now only a small square building, like an old warehouse, with rust on its corrugated steel roof and ivy creeping up the walls. Inside there was nothing but some bags of concrete and a few moldy blankets.

Harley stood at the edge of the parking area. She stared at the place where the vast room had been, the place where she had seen her father emerging from a sphere of light. "How could they do this?" she asked, tears springing to her eyes. "How could they get rid of everything so quickly?"

Noah shook his head. "I don't know. It doesn't seem possible."

"How are we going to find my father?" Harley asked, wiping her eyes with her sleeve. She felt tired, overwhelmed, and lost. This empty base seemed somehow more terrible than anything else they had seen.

Noah moved over and put his arm gently around her shoulders. "We'll have to find Cain—or wait until he finds us. He's the only connection we have to any of this. And I know I have a *lot* of questions for that guy."

"Do you think Cain was telling the truth?" Harley asked softly. "Is my father really part of Unit 17?"

Noah shrugged. "I don't know."

"And what about the things that Josh said?" asked Harley. "About you being placed with your family and having so much *potential*. Potential for *what*?"

"I don't know that, either," Noah replied. "And I don't know what Josh and Coach Rocklin even *are*. And I surely don't know why anyone—or any*thing*—would bother implanting a transmitter in my back." He turned her toward him and stared into her eyes with brave determination. "But I'm going to find out."

"How?" Harley wanted to believe Noah, but she could feel her last glimmers of hope fading fast. "How do you plan to do that?"

He shook his head. "I'm not sure yet. But I don't think our answers are here." He released Harley and walked toward his car. "Come on. Let's go find them."

Harley took one last look around the base. Whomever had made the base disappear had done an excellent job of not leaving a single clue to where they'd gone. They wanted her to give up—to relinquish all hope.

Harley squinted at the empty field all around her and set her mouth in a firm line. She wouldn't give up. She'd gone through too much, and she knew, deep down inside, that her father was still out there—somewhere. And he needed her. "I'll find the truth," she said as strongly as she could manage. "No matter what it takes."

She climbed into the car alongside Noah. The Mustang growled to life and they drove away.

At the edge of the woods, a red glow shone between the black winter trees. It drifted along for a few moments, trailing behind the car. Then it drifted back into the forest.

Everything was quiet.

To be continued . . .